Dinah Maria Mulock Craik

Concerning Men and Other Papers

Dinah Maria Mulock Craik

Concerning Men and Other Papers

ISBN/EAN: 9783337279486

Printed in Europe, USA, Canada, Australia, Japan

Cover: Foto ©Andreas Hilbeck / pixelio.de

More available books at **www.hansebooks.com**

CONCERNING MEN

AND OTHER PAPERS

CONCERNING MEN

AND OTHER PAPERS

BY THE AUTHOR OF

'JOHN HALIFAX, GENTLEMAN'

London
MACMILLAN AND CO.
AND NEW YORK
1888

These were the last papers Mrs. Craik wrote. She intended to collect and republish them with others that were never written, but only planned.

CONTENTS

CONCERNING MEN

I HAVE been asked to write a paper giving a woman's opinions upon men ; the reason urged for this request being ' that a woman who has for the purposes of literary art analysed the minds of men and women must have reached valuable conclusions as to the mutual limitations of each sex, and its supplementation by the other.'

It may be so. One cannot have written novels for forty years without much study and observation of human character, to say nothing of the inevitable experience which a long life brings. And yet I have hesitated. We all know ourselves better than outsiders do, and I am conscious of having lived, in a

B

sense, out of the world—a quiet happy domestic existence, which never brought me in
contact with really bad men. Consequently,
pessimistic or Zolaesque studies of them had
no charm for me ; and I have shared with
many other female writers the accusation
that all my men are 'women's men,' *i.e.* men,
painted, not as they are, but after the ideal—
a woman's ideal—of what they ought to be.
Perhaps we might retort how very little men
know of us, and how unlike to real women
are the heroines of many male novelists.
The difference seems to be, that a woman's
man is generally gifted with impossible virtues,
while a man's woman, if not enchantingly
wicked, is often so tame and weak, even
silly, like Thackeray's *Amelia* and a dozen
more I could name, that the best of her sex
would be ashamed to own her.

Be that as it may, I will not argue the
question ; I have been asked to say my say,

and I say it, without dogmatism, but also without fear.

It is as well to premise, however, that all my observations and experience of life have confirmed me in one belief, viz. that while, as a rule, the average woman is superior to the average man,—more estimable, lovable—nay, often more capable and reliable,—there are exceptional men nobler than any woman; for the simple reason that the masculine nature is larger and stronger, with wider possibilities for both evil and good.

> All thy passions, matched with mine,
> Are like moonlight unto sunlight and as water unto
>   wine,

is a truth affirmed by a wise man, which should never be ignored in a woman's judgment of men.

Also, though we find continual exceptions —women as strong as many a man, and men tenderer than most women—still the creed that 'woman is the lesser man' does in the main hold good, intellectually as well as physically. Morally, I doubt. In purity, single-mindedness, unselfishness, faithfulness, the ordinary man is distinctly below the ordinary woman. You would have but to look in, Asmodeus-like, upon any fifty households of your acquaintance, comparing the husbands with the wives, the brothers with the sisters, in their internal and domestic, not their outside society life, to be pretty sure that such is the case. But, as I shall presently show, this is mainly the women's fault.

It is better to bow before an unseen divinity than to adore the fish-bone fetish of a South Sea Islander; therefore, if I judge severely men as they are, it is because I have never swerved from my belief in what they are capable of, or my early ideal of what they ought to be.

Much as has been said about the equality of the sexes, and great as is the indignation of some of us at being considered 'the weaker sex,' I am afraid that absolute equality between men and women is impossible. Nature herself sets her face against it ; and chiefly by the desire implanted in most women's breasts to look up, physically and mentally, to some one greater than themselves ; unto whom they can cling, and on whom they can rely, without any sense of inferiority. Not merely to love but to worship, to make herself a mat for the man's feet to walk over, to believe everything he does and says is right, to be ready to live for him or die for him, and merge her own identity completely in his—this, I think, is the instinct of most women, or at least the noblest half of them. It is Nature ; and Nature, we must allow, is occasionally right.

Nature, too, lays down limits beyond which

women, in the aggregate, cannot pass. She means them to be—not men, or rather imitation men, but the mothers of men. I am old-fashioned enough to believe that every girl's education, mental, moral, physical, ought to be primarily with a view to wifehood and motherhood, the highest and happiest destiny to which any woman can attain. Even when Fate denies them this chiefest blessing—as, considering the large surplus female population in the world, must often be the case—she still leaves them the possibility of being the spiritual mothers of a new generation—as maiden aunts, Sisters in Orphanages, hospital nurses, and the like. While sufficient to themselves, able to do their own work in the world, solitary but strong—unmarried women may still keep up, as many an old maid does keep up, the natural maternal instinct, by helping all helpless creatures and becoming an ennobling influence to mankind in the aggregate, if not to the individual man.

This abstract mother-impulse, absent in the other sex—a man loves his own children, but seldom any other man's—is, I believe, the keynote of feminine nature, and has its roots in distinct psychological and physiological laws. Man is made of muscle and brains; by them he has to govern the world. His very selfishness, or, call it selfism, his hardness and masterfulness, are, in one sense, a necessity, else he would never be able to fight his way and protect those whom he is bound to protect. But woman's kingdom is the heart. A woman without tenderness, without gentleness, without the power of self-suppression to an almost infinite degree, is a creature so anomalous that she cannot fail to do enormous harm, both to her own sex and to the other. She ceases to be the guardian angel she was meant to be, and becomes an angel-faced devil, working woe wherever she appears.

One often hears girls, and very good girls too, declaring that 'they like men far better than women,' and putting in mankind a sublime impossible trust, which if the other sex justified, we should have no 'strong-minded' women. It is the reaction after loss, the unfaith which follows on broken idols, which makes a great many foolish women join in the howl against men. They begin by being blind worshippers, and end either as rebels or slaves. Only a very few have courage to take the medium course, and, while refusing either to adore or condemn, content themselves with simply loving; a wise, open-eyed love, which sees faults even in the best-beloved, and, loving still, steadily tries to amend them.

For many of the sins of mankind women have themselves to blame. First, for their viciousness and coarseness, women being either too ignorant or too cowardly to exact from men the same standard of virtue which men expect from them. Secondly, for their tyranny, because the laws and customs of many generations have placed women far too much in the power of men ; and even were it not so, their own warm affections make them too easy slaves. Thirdly, for the selfishness which — doubtless with righteous reason— is so deeply implanted in the masculine breast, that a thoroughly unselfish man is almost a *lusus naturæ*. And no wonder, since from his cradle his womenkind have adored him. Mothers, nurses, sisters, all join in the sweet flattery, the perpetual acquiescence, which make him, as boy and man, think far too much of himself. Then, perhaps, comes a period of innocent tyranny from his sweetheart, which he soon repays by tyrannising over his wife. Thus, except that brief season when Love has

Struck the chord of self, which, trembling, passed
in music out of sight,

there is, for the ordinary man—I do not say
the ideal man, or even the specially good
man—no time in his life when he is not
bolstered up in his only too natural egotism
by the foolish subservience or adoring love-
servitude of the women about him.

Loving and serving is a woman's destiny,
but it should be done in a right way. To
yield to a man when you know he is in
the wrong, to teach others that he must be
yielded to whether right or wrong, is to place
him on a pedestal where not one man in
twenty thousand could stand steady. The
unspoken creed of many a household, especially in the last generation, that the girls must
always give in to the boys, that endless
money should be spent on the boys' education and career in the world, while the girls
must shift for themselves—this it is, I believe,

which has brought about that painful reaction, in which women are gradually unsexing themselves, trying to do a multitude of things which Nature never meant them to do, and losing sight of that which she did mean, viz. that they should be, first the wives and mothers, and, failing that, the friends, consolers, and helpers of men.

This they can be in a hundred ways, without attempting the impossible, and without controverting the supposed Christian doctrine that the man is the head of the woman; as he ought to be if he deserves it, but which when truly deserving he will seldom obnoxiously claim to be. It is a curious fact, which I have noticed throughout my life, that the strongest, noblest, wisest men are those who are the least afraid of granting to women all the 'rights' they could possibly desire, and the most generous in allowing them all the qualities, so often dormant through neglected education, which they possess in common with men.

One of these, strange as it may appear, is the 'business faculty,' usually attributed to men only—except in France, where, especially among the *bourgeoisie,* 'Madame' does the business of the family, which prospers accordingly. Despite her revolutions there is no richer, more economical, nor more thriving country than France, and none where women do more work or are more highly regarded.

'I would never let my daughter marry an Englishman,' said to me once a French lady, a better 'business woman' and doing daily more practical work than most men; 'vos maris Anglais sont toujours tyrans.' I hope not! but I think English husbands and fathers would be wiser if, instead of saying contemptuously that 'women never understand business,' they taught their womenkind to understand it. This would lighten their own hands amazingly, take from them half the worries which convert them into supposed 'tyrants,' besides being an incalculable advantage to the women themselves.

Men, from their large *ego*, have a tendency to take interest chiefly in their own affairs, to see things solely from their own point of view, and to judge things, not as they are, but as the world will look at them with reference to their individual selves. But their power and inclination to take trouble are rarely equal to a woman's. Her very narrowness makes her more conscientious and reliable in matters of minute detail. A man's horizon is wider, his vision larger, his physical and intellectual strength generally greater than a woman's; but he is as a rule less prudent, less careful, less able to throw himself out of himself, and into the interests of other people. Granted a capable woman, and one who has had even a tithe of the practical education that all men have or are supposed to have, she will do a matter of business, say an executorship, secretaryship, etc., as well as any man, or even better than most men, because she will take more pains.

Did girls get from childhood the same business training as boys, and were it clearly understood in all families that it is no credit but rather a discredit for women to hang helpless on the men instead of doing their own work, and if necessary earning their own living, I believe society would be not the worse but the better for the change. Men would find out that the more they elevate women the greater use they get out of them. If instead of a man working himself to death for his unmarried daughters, and then leaving them ignominiously dependent upon male relations, he educated them to independence, made them able both to maintain and to protect themselves, it would save him and them a world of unhappiness. They would cease to be either the rivals—a very hopeless rivalry —or the playthings first and afterwards the slaves of men ; and become, as was originally intended, their co-mates, equal and yet different, each sex supplying the other's deficiencies, and therefore fitted to work together, not apart, for the good of the world.

What this work should be, individual capacity alone must decide. There are so many things which women cannot do, that I think men would be wise as well as just in letting them do whatever they can do. As clerks, bookkeepers, secretaries, poor-law guardians, superintendents of hospitals and similar institutions, they would, if properly trained, be quite as capable as men. The oft-repeated cry that thereby they lower the rate of wages and take the bread out of men's mouths is only that of feeble fear. Women must either be maintained or maintain themselves ; it is no injury but a relief to men when those to whom Providence has not given the blessed duties of wives and mothers do maintain themselves, in any lawful and possible way.

So many ways are to them absolutely impossible. They cannot be soldiers, sailors, or enter on any profession which entails violent physical exertion or endurance. Mentally, too, their powers are limited. Exceptional female brains there are, equal to male, but I believe the average young woman would never go through the curriculum of our public schools and colleges without serious harm, especially to that nervous organisation which is far more delicate than that of the average young man, and to the general health which is so important not only to herself but to the next generation. 'Send me,' wrote a colonial bishop in want of missionary help, 'send me a cargo of capable *old maids.*' But any career which young maidens are put to which is likely to unfit them for their natural destiny, as mothers of the men and women to be, must be injurious to the future of the world.

Therefore, in one profession where men have exceedingly resented our entrance, great caution is required that it should be entered solely by exceptional women, gifted not only with masculine aspirations but masculine strength, mental and physical—I mean the medical profession. Nevertheless, to exclude them altogether would be a great mistake. Whether women could ever make as good doctors as men, *i.e.* general practitioners, consulting physicians, surgeons or scientists, is very doubtful; but there is one branch of the profession which in modern times men have taken to themselves, and which women would do well to take back again into their own hands. Obstetric practice once did belong, and still ought to belong, exclusively

C

to capable, carefully trained, and experienced medical *women*. No medical man, with his many daily cases of ordinary illness—often infectious illness—and his very limited time, ought to have anything to do with that crisis which requires patience, caution, prudence, and above all no hurry or worry. I believe the number of women, especially poor women, who have been actually murdered through having male attendance in their hour of need, would, if known, be enough argument for our sex to hold its own, and, on this point at least, stand by one another, and educate a phalanx of capable *accoucheuses* who should effectually absorb this branch of the medical profession, leaving to men all the rest.

Few, at best, will be the number of women who have brains, will, and physical stamina enough to compete with men in the arena of the world, fewer still those who have any wish to do it. Half of us would rather stay at home and do our work, domestic work; the other and inferior half prefer to let the man work, while they run about and enjoy themselves. But such exceptional women as have masculine aspirations and masculine capacities may safely be allowed to use the one and gratify the other. There will always be enough of us left who are content to be mere daughters, sisters, wives and mothers, willing to merge ourselves in the men we love, to spend and be spent for them, often with small thanks and no reward, except the comfort of knowing that they could not well do without us, and that after all it does not much matter which does the work of life, so that it is done.

That as a whole men do it better than we, is, I think, a mistake. Their labours are seen, ours unseen. Their aims are larger, perhaps nobler, but they are less persistent than we are; more prone to get 'weary of well doing.' In physical courage they excel us, but in moral courage I think very few men are equal to women. (The reader must pardon this continual repetition of 'I think' and 'I believe,' necessary in some way to neutralise the sweeping dogmatism which is at once so odious and so difficult to avoid.) Arrant cowards as many of us are in the matter of our affections, ready to do anything rather than contradict a bad-tempered husband or vex a disagreeable brother, when it comes to any great moral heroism, or that endurance which is often greater than heroism, there are few men so strong and brave as a woman. It is well known in the statistics of lunatic asylums that the largest proportion of male patients have been driven mad by worldly misfortunes. Not so with us. We can endure almost any amount of external suffering ; stand on our feet and support others. The thing which breaks our hearts and turns our brains is, as statistics also prove, inward anguish. We can endure life and face death, but our one vulnerable point is our affections.

It seems as if this paper 'concerning men' were drifting into an essay upon women, yet both are so inevitably mixed up together that it is difficult to divide them. But there is one point of difference between men and women which I ought not quite to pass over, and yet shall not dilate upon, for I believe no woman is capable of fairly judging it. Mercifully for the world, very few women can in the least understand that side of men's nature, in which the senses predominate over or are perpetually fighting with the soul, so that an originally noble human being can sink down to the level of Calypso's swine. I question if even an ordinary woman—being a good woman—can realise the state of mind which results in a man's making some wretched *mésalliance*, or sinking under the unlawful thraldom of a Cleopatra, an Aspasia, or a Phryne. Such things are, but most of us women can hardly comprehend them. We may, under some extraordinary self-delusion, fall in love with a bad man and cling to him from duty or tenderness long after love has departed ; but we seldom plunge as a man does, open-eyed, into the nets spread by a bad woman, whom he knows to be a bad woman, and yet cannot help himself. The story of Samson and Delilah, repeated age after age among men, is not often told of us women.

Nor is this common in lesser forms of folly or guilt. If we sin, it is generally through self-deception, but men do it with their eyes open. I remember once at a dinner-party hearing my host piteously lamenting over his gout, because of which his doctor had prohibited wine. Immediately afterwards I saw him toss off a bumper of champagne. 'Why do you do that?' I asked. 'Oh, because,' he hesitated, 'because I can't help it.' He is dead now, but before his death his splendid fortune had all melted away, and his wife and children were earning their daily bread. And why? Because of that miserable contemptible 'can't help it.' Now, if there is one thing in which the average woman is superior to the average man, it is because she generally *can* 'help it.'

But, I repeat, some, nay, many men are found nobler than the very noblest of women. One perhaps toils all his life at a trade he hates, yet which happens to be the only calling in which he can earn the family bread; another resigns silently all the lawful pleasures of existence, intellectual and social, to that same cruel necessity of providing for his dear ones; a third, year after year, endures with sublime patience the fretfulness of an invalid

wife or the sin and misery of a drunken one.
A fourth, less wretched than these, yet still
most unfortunate, having married from gratitude or impulse, still year after year honourably and faithfully puts up with the companionship of a woman who is no companion
at all, with whom he has not the slightest
sympathy, whom he either never loved rightly
or has long ceased to love; yet for a whole
lifetime he hides this fact and its consequences
in his own bosom, without ever letting the
world find out, or guess that he himself has
found out, what he now knows to have been
a terrible mistake.   Such instances, not rare,
are enough to prove even to the most virulent
of his feminine detractors that man, 'made in
the image of God,' has something godlike
about him still, something that we women
are justified in admiring and adoring; devot-
ing, nay, sacrificing ourselves to him, as I am
afraid we shall do to the end of the chapter.

But the sacrifice ought to be a just and right one, else it is worse than useless—sinful. Any self-devotion which makes its object selfish and conceited, as a man can scarcely fail to be with a circle of women blindly worshipping him ; any foolish tenderness which, instead of strengthening, weakens him ; any slavish fear which rouses all his dormant love of power into positive tyranny,—these things are in us women not virtues but vices. A certain novel lately published, entitled *This Man's Wife*, in which a 'pattern' woman believes blindly for about twenty years in a villain of a husband, sacrificing to him her father and mother, her child, two faithful friends, once lovers, and herself, is a picture that outrages all one's notions of commonsense and justice, and when the woman dies at last one is inclined to say, not 'What a martyr !' but 'What a fool !'

The relation between men and women

ought to be as equal and as righteous as their love; also as clear-sighted, that by means of it each may educate and elevate the other; both looking beyond each other to that absolute right and perfect love, without which all human love must surely soon or late melt away in disenchantment, distaste, or even actual dislike. For love can die—there is no truth more certain and more terrible; and each human being that lives carries within himself or herself the possibility of being its murderer.

It will be seen that in all my judgments I have held a medium course, because, to me at least, this appears the only one possible. Neither sex can benefit by over-exalting or lowering the other. They are meant to work together, side by side, for mutual help and comfort, each tacitly supplying the other's deficiencies, without recriminations, or discussions as to what qualities are or are not possessed by either. The instant they begin to fight about their separate rights they are almost sure to forget their mutual duties, which are much more important to the conservation of society.

For—let them argue as they will—neither can do without the other; and though, as I remember once hearing or reading, it is most true that only at one special time of life are they absolutely essential each to each, that after the heyday of youth has gone by, most men prefer the society of men, and women of women—except of the one, if ever found, who is its other half, its 'spirit's mate, compassionate and wise '—still, in most lives, and above all in married lives, a man is to a woman and a woman to a man, even when all passion has died out, a stronghold, a completeness, such as no two women or two men ever can be to one another. The Maker of all things made it so, and we cannot alter it.

To sum up, I fear that, argue as we may, we shall never arrive at any clearer elucidation of this great mystery than the eminently practical one conveyed in most perfect poetry by one of the wisest of our century, whose serene old age will only confirm the belief of his ardent youth.   It is Alfred Tennyson who tells us that women and men are

> Not like to like, but like in difference,
> Yet in the long years liker they must grow ;
> The man be more of woman, she of man—
> He gain in sweetness and in moral height,
> Nor lose the wrestling thews that throw the world ;
> She mental breadth, nor fail in child-ward care,
> Nor lose the childlike in the larger mind.
> Till at the last she set herself to man,
> Like perfect music unto noble words.

FOR BETTER FOR WORSE

'FOR better for worse.' How many young
creatures repeat these words, unthinkingly,
or thinking that the future will be all better
and no worse—that marriage is a kind of
earthly paradise, and those only are to be
pitied who stand without the gate. They
are ; for a single life is necessarily an im-
perfect life. But a perfect married life,
though there is such a thing, is the rarest
thing under the sun. Of the thousands who
have known the rapture of love, even of
satisfied love, there are only tens, nay units,
who live to know what the poet calls 'comfort of marriage' — the unity of interests,
the entire reliance, the constant, faithful

companionship; the peaceful habitual affection which replaces passion; which month after month, year after year, sits every day at the same board, and lays the tired head every night on the same pillow, quite certain and quite content in that certainty, that nothing but the inevitable 'till death us do part' will ever involve separation.

It is only those who understand and believe in such marriage who have a right to speak on a much-discussed subject, which has been viewed in many phases, but all chiefly from the worldly side—the man's side. I wish to say a word or two on the moral and spiritual side—and the woman's.

There is a difference between the two. A man makes his own marriage. It is he who is supposed to take the initiative: to woo, ask, and win. If the union turns out a mistake, he has, ordinarily, no one to blame but himself. But there are myriads of women who, by persuasion of friends, or of the lover himself, by the self-delusion and self-sacrifice which ' the weaker sex ' is constantly prone to, from poverty, pride, or disappointed affections, and other less pitiable and more ignoble motives—marry in haste and repent at leisure; wake up from a temporary hallucination to find themselves in the position of a creature fallen into a bog, where the more it struggles the deeper it sinks. All the deeper that its struggles are, for the most part, dumb.

Not always. It is a curious fact that while a man who has made an unfortunate marriage is generally totally silent on the subject, women, if they utter no open outcry, often secretly complain, and those most who have the least to complain of. For such there need not be felt the slightest pity. If their life is destroyed, they destroy it themselves; not merely by the first foolish step—which many take, for the average of marriages are not ideal, but result only in a convenient mutual toleration—but because they will not make the best of things, will not take in the vital truth that happiness — or perhaps I should say blessedness—consists, not in obtaining what we crave for, but in turning to noble uses that which we have.

Many a wife goes about making 'a poor mouth' about mere trifles. Her husband has not given her the position she expected; he likes town and she the country, or *vice versâ ;* he has a good heart but a bad temper; his relatives are unpleasant, or he takes a dislike, just or unjust, to hers; all these minor miseries silly women dwell upon, instead of accepting them, like the husband, 'for better for worse,' and striving by all conceivable means, by patience, by self-denial, by courage when necessary, and by silent endurance always, to change worse into better. This can be done, and often is done. If we, who have lived long enough to look on life with larger eyes than the young, are often saddened to see how many of the most passionate love - marriages melt away into a middle age of misery, we have also seen others which, beginning in error, and possessing all the elements of future wretchedness, have yet by wise conduct—generally on the wife's side — ended in something not far short of happiness.

Every woman who takes upon herself the 'holy estate'—and it is indeed holy—'of matrimony' has to learn soon or late—happy if she learn it soon!—that no two human beings can be tied together for life without finding endless difficulties, not only in the world outside, but in each other. These have to be solved, and generally by the wife. She must have a strong heart, a sweet temper, an unlimited patience, and above all,

D

a power to see the right, and do it, not merely for the love of man — 'as Sarah obeyed Abraham, calling him Lord' (a state of things belonging to a polygamous and not a Christian community)—but for the love of God, which alone can tide an ill-assorted couple over the rocks and quicksands of early married life into a calm sea and a prosperous voyage.

I state this, that if what I am about to say be somewhat iconoclastic, it should be clearly seen that I wage war against false idols and not against true gods. And I write, not for those whose matrimonial lot is the average one, neither very happy nor very miserable, who having made their bed must lie upon it and make the best of it; but for those whose lot has turned out—as the man said of his bad wife —'all worse and no better,' who are tied and bound, not always by their own fault, with a ghastly

chain, the iron of which enters their very
soul, and from which ·they have no hope of
escape but death.

The question I wish to raise is, how long
a woman should endure that chain ; how far
she may righteously put up with the husband,
whom, under whatever circumstances, she has
taken ' for better for worse,' and found hopelessly 'worse.' The opposite question, as to
how a good man should deal with a bad wife,
I do not enter into. Men are the law-makers,
and can be trusted to take care of themselves.

In ancient times most nations were polygamous, including the Jews, upon whose
marriage laws ours—rightly or wrongly—are
founded ; witness St. Paul's advice on the
text of Sarah—' whose daughters ye are '—
in our marriage homily. Women were held
to be the mere goods and chattels, first of
father, then of husband, and bought and sold
accordingly. Early Christianity, while rais-

ing the woman to the level of being 'one flesh' with the man, absorbed her in him, as 'bone of *his* bone and flesh of *his* flesh,' giving her few or no rights of her own. Only of late years has she been recognised as a separate entity, with feelings, duties, rights ; man's partner and helpmeet, but in no sense his slave, as, though outwardly treated as a goddess, she really was throughout all the Middle Ages of Europe. Now, public opinion has changed. The much-lauded 'Patient Griseldis' would be scouted in most modern society as a woman whose conduct showed a cowardice absolutely criminal ; and in many honest minds even Tennyson's lovely story of 'Enid and Geraint' leaves an ugly doubt behind whether the man was not a brute and the woman a simpleton.

Yet still, despite advancing civilisation, there is in some people a lurking feeling for the brute and against the simpleton ; a clinging to the letter of the law—'Those whom God hath joined together let no man put asunder'—forgetting that many marriages seem made not by God, but, if I may say it, by the devil. Even the marriage service itself warns us that 'as many as are coupled together otherwise than as God's word doth allow, are not joined together by Him, neither is their matrimony lawful.'

There are many marriages which, 'if the secrets of all hearts were disclosed'—I quote still from the marriage service—are unlawful from the first; and many more that become unlawful afterwards, to continue in which is far more sinful than to break them. Besides infidelity, the one cause for which law, though, I shame to say, not always social opinion or custom, justifies a woman in quitting her husband, there are other wrongs, equally cruel, and equally fatal in result, which Society allows her to endure to the bitter end.　A man may be a confirmed drunkard, a spendthrift, a liar—a scoundrel so complete that no honest gentleman would admit him within his doors; and yet the wretched woman his wife is expected to 'do her duty'—to 'stick to him through thick and thin'—so goes the phrase.　She must shut her eyes to all his sins, and make believe to herself and the world at large that none exist; continue to 'obey him and serve him' according to her marriage vow; be the mistress of his house, and—most terrible fate of all!—the mother of his children.　And the world, even the virtuous half of it, will uphold and praise her, affirming that she only does what every loyal wife ought to do—and is quite right to do it.

I say she is wrong—culpably wrong; that her noble endurance, falsely so called, is mere cowardice, and her conjugal submission a degradation as sinful as that of many a

woman who omits the marriage ceremony altogether. A woman, married to a thoroughly
bad man, and making believe that he is a
good man, must be either a hypocrite, lost to
all sense of right and wrong—or a fool. Her
patience is an error, her self-sacrifice a crime,
for neither ends with herself alone.

And here I draw the line—which law as
well as public opinion ought to draw—where
endurance is bound to end. A childless wife
may, if she chooses, immolate herself, like a
Hindoo widow, in the moral suttee which
many good people still hold to as a part of
the Christian religion; but when she is a
mother, the case is totally different. There
is one 'cause for which marriage was or-
dained'—I still quote from the Prayer-book
—which has been overlooked by our legis-
lators—namely, the children.

The divorce laws in all countries make
the grounds of separation personal between

husband and wife, and the question of duty is held to lie solely with these two. Whereas, for both, and beyond both, is a higher duty still—that which they, and Society, owe to the innocent creatures whom marriage has brought into the world; who did not ask to be born, and yet must support existence, tainted by the sins and darkened by the sufferings of parents who primarily never thought of them at all.

I may startle many by affirming that the first duty of every woman who deliberately chooses the lot of Mother Eve is—her children. Nature herself upholds this law. In most brute beasts, from the time the double life begins the mother is wholly a mother—and solely; the father having nothing at all to do with his offspring. Higher forms of existence recognise the double parental tie; but still the claim of child upon mother and mother upon child, begun through physical sufferings and joys of which men are equally ignorant, and continued through years of patient care of which they are in general quite incapable, constitutes a bond like nothing else in the world. I do not hesitate to say that it is a closer bond and a stronger duty than that towards any husband; unless it be a husband who fulfils all *his* duties, and is as truly a father as the mother is, or ought to be—a mother. And when these two duties clash, as duties often do in this world, I believe the mother ought to choose first the duty to her children. A man can take care of himself—can ruin or save himself; for, however she may imagine it, very seldom can any woman save a thoroughly bad husband. Nor, though she married him, is she responsible for him, beyond a certain extent; she is responsible for her children from the hour of birth—nay, for the very fact of their existence.

It would be entering on too wide a field of discussion to open the question whether those who are stricken with any hereditary taint should marry, or be allowed to marry, at all. And this paper is meant to deal with a woman's position and duty after marriage; when time has proved without doubt that the marriage was not 'made in Heaven,' but—in the other place. Is she justified in destroying not only herself but her helpless children in that hell upon earth which a bad man can create around him by his unrestrained vices?

That word *vices* answers the question. No mere fault or misfortune, such as incompatibility of temper, hopeless sickness, or worldly ruin, does in the least abrogate that solemn covenant 'for better for worse'—but vice does. Confirmed drunkenness, evil courses of any kind, ingrained lack of principle, cruel tyranny, and that violent temper that is akin to madness and equally dangerous—whatever compels a woman to teach her children that to serve God they must *not* imitate their father, warrants her in quitting him and taking them from him. Whenever things come to that pass that the vileness of the father will destroy the children, physically and morally, then the mother's course is clear. She must save them, nor suffer their father's sins to blight their whole future existence.

For—let me dare to utter the plain truth —they ought never to have existed at all. To make a drunkard, a debauchee, a scoundrel of any sort, the father of her children, is, to a righteous woman, a sin almost equivalent to child-murder. And she slays not only their bodies but their souls ; entailing on them an hereditary curse, which may not be rooted out for generations.

Therefore, for any good woman married to a scoundrel there is but one duty—separation. Not divorce. This, by permitting re-marriage, which the victim would seldom or never desire, would allow the victimiser to carry into a new home the misery he has inflicted on the former one. But legal separation—*a mensâ et thoro*—giving to the wife exactly the position of a widow, and to the children the safety of being fatherless, for a bad father is worse than none—ought to be easily and cheaply attainable by all classes.

The question of income and maintenance would have its difficulties ; but, as a general rule, a wife who thus voluntarily leaves her husband should only take away with her what is absolutely her own. She wishes to be freed from himself ; she does not want his money. Also, though this may sometimes fall hard, I think the support of the children should devolve upon her. This removes the possibility of mercenary or worldly or vicious motives for the separation, and places it entirely on moral grounds. Money, wrung legally out of a bad father, would, in most women's eyes, only bring a curse with it; and there are few mothers who, if put to the test, would not prefer the hardest poverty for themselves and their children, rather than the misery of a home in which the name of husband and father is a mere sham; where— sharpest pang of all—they have to sit still and see their little ones slowly contaminated by one to whom the hapless innocents owe nothing but the mere accident of existence.

By the outside world this condition of quasi-widowhood, if sad and difficult, should be held in no way dishonourable. To it would attach none of the degradations and foul revelations of divorce; indeed, the fact that separation was easy would make divorce all the more difficult, as should be. Easy divorce loosens all the rivets which hold society together, and, while giving no consolation to innocence, offers a premium to guilt. The great safeguard of marriage is its inevitableness; the consciousness that no power on earth can ever place either party in the same position as before their union. Otherwise, only too many couples would separate in the first year of their union. But the mistake, known to be irrevocable, is borne, and sometimes partially remedied. When irremediable, the utmost that both parties can expect and most would desire, is to get free from one another—as free as they can, and save their children from the consequences of their fatal error.

This, and no more than this, I think they have a right to. Neither law nor public opinion can place, or ought to place, unhappy married couples in the same position as if they had never committed that false step. One can deeply pity a woman whose husband is transported for forgery, or a man whose wife is shut up permanently in a lunatic asylum ; but, though these things involve and justify a life-long separation, they would form a ghastly and dangerous argument for divorce. Nay, speaking as a woman, and for women, I doubt if divorce should ever be permissible. Few of us would either care to become the wife of a divorced man, or feel it right to marry at all while the husband, the father of our children, was still alive.

But the spectacle of a woman who refuses to condone vice and perpetuate evil, who has strength to cut off a right hand and put out a right eye, rather than sin against God and ruin the young souls He has entrusted to her, would be deterrent rather than dangerous. Many a man, who, knowing his wife dare not or cannot leave him, is selfish, tyrannical, brutal, breaking every law of God and man except those for which he would be openly punished, if he thought she *would* leave him—

could get rid of him by means short of divorce, and without the odium to herself and the freedom to him that result from divorce,— would possibly amend his ways. If not, he would richly deserve the justice without mercy — for mercy to the sinful is often mercilessness to the innocent — which is Society's only safeguard against such men. They are not fit for domestic life ; and, though in public life some of them brazen it out to the last, the best that Society can do for them is to save other women from them, help their wives to gather together the fragments of a wrecked existence, and teach their children to cover over with wise and duteous silence the very name of father.

There are fathers—and fathers. Those who deserve the name will not resent my distinguishing between them. And no good husband is harmed by laws which protect hapless women against bad husbands. On the other hand, there are women as unfit to be mothers as wives, and God help the man who has chosen such an one! But, as I have said, the choice is his own; he is—apparently, at least—the active, not the passive agent in his own hard fate. And he generally bears it in heroic silence. So should she. If, refusing to lower her womanhood by continuing to live with a bad man, she has courage to quit him, she deserves not merely pity but respect. But she deserves neither, if, while tamely submitting to her misery, she raises a feeble wailing or a monstrous howling against it. Such women encourage bad men, and injure good men by appealing to the noblest quality of the stronger sex—compassion.

It is to obviate this, to set up a standard by which good men can fairly judge good women, that I write the present paper; starting with the principle that in most cases of

E

unhappy marriage the first thing to be considered is *the good of the children.*　Secondly, that while divorce, being undesirable in itself, and dangerous to the community at large, should be made as difficult as possible, separation, restoring to both parties all rights which they had before marriage, except that of remarrying, should be made easily and honourably obtainable.

What men should do in a similar case, I leave to themselves to say.　I speak only for women, hoping my words may strengthen some of them to break through that cruel bondage of body and soul, ending in untold misery— nay, worse than misery, guilt— caused by the false interpretation that so many well-meaning, narrow-minded people put upon the words—most sacred words to all who really understand them !—'*for better for worse.*'

A HOUSE OF REST

I HAVE always had a strong feeling—looking back, I may say a fellow-feeling, for our respectable poor : those who, well-born, fairly well-educated, with all the tastes and instincts of refinement, have been reduced, sometimes by their own fault, more often by the faults of their progenitors, not merely to earn their bread, for that is a wholesome and most desirable thing, but to earn it so hardly that existence becomes one long struggle—especially to women. For, in their case, the struggle is mostly a silent one. The clamourers are heard and helped. Our unrespectable poor, who have no longer any position to keep up ; our criminal classes, whom it is

so 'interesting' to try and reform ; and the
multitudes of helpless ones, the old, the very
young, the sick, can each and all find an institution on the watch to succour them.   But
those who are ashamed to beg, and too proud
even to complain, determined to keep 'respectable' through everything, just go working
on—work till they drop.   And this class is
mainly composed of women.   Because, whatever used to be, there is no doubt that now a
large proportion of our women never are,
never can be, worked for.   They must work
for themselves, or starve.   Often, they do
both ; and no one knows it, till they 'die and
make no sign.'   For it is beginning to be
generally recognised by philanthropists—
notably by the philanthropists of the East
End of London—that public charity often
flows in the direction least needed and merited ;
because the deserving poor are almost always
the silent poor.

Nothing but experience, or very close observation, can teach one to realise the position of a woman, usually a young woman—for such seldom reach old age—who day after day must put on decent clothes and a cheerful, or at any rate a calm face, and, sick or well, glad or sorry, go about her daily work, without intermission, or thought of intermission, knowing well that there is absolutely nothing but that work between her and hunger. The craving for rest, the terror of 'breaking down'—the natural youthful longing for a little pleasure, a little happiness, all have to be set aside. To the working girl, shop-girl or needle-woman, it is work—work — work, for ever, except for four days (bank holidays) and two weeks once a year ; and very thankful, the world says, ought the girl to be, that she gets work to do at all.

Granted !—and yet——

My tenderly-reared and charming young lady, with your lessons and your play, your lawn-tennis, your dancing and your skating —pretty clothes to wear and smiling parents to come to the rescue, should your allowance run short — plenty of companions, and perhaps a lover in the distance; can you imagine what it is to rise up every morning and work till night? to live in close rooms and sleep in closer ones, thankful for any solitude? or else to inhabit a single room, and have nothing but your own dreary company from morning till night? no family to amuse you, no parents to fly to for help? Or, equally sad, perhaps, not a soul whom *you* can help;—and, indeed, having enough to do to keep your own body and soul together, upon the proceeds of that continuous toil which makes your eyes ache and your senses swim? Do you, my lovely young friend, when you are trying on a new dress, ever turn for a minute and look at the face of the girl who tries it on ?

She is probably a very well-dressed and fine-looking girl, almost as much a lady in externals as you are yourself; but there is sometimes a look in her face which your mother would not like to see in yours. She wants *rest*—rest of body and mind ; a little pause in the grinding of that terrible mill which grinds—not old people young, but young people old, preternaturally, cruelly old.

It may seem a harsh doctrine, but I believe the lowest class of the poor, long accustomed to live from hand to mouth, to feast to-day and starve to-morrow, to clamour incessantly for charity, and often to prefer it to work, do really suffer much less than the class above them. By a long course of hardening they have ceased to feel either the ugliness or the degradation of poverty ;

their physical as well as their moral percep-
tions are blunted ; they are not nearly so
much to be pitied as their helpers suppose.
Yet for them help is seldom wanting.
Workhouse treats, Ragged School feasts,
teas for Midnight Refuges and suppers for
thieves, Reformatories for young criminals,
and Prisoners' Aid Societies for elder ones
—this is as it should be. But may I say a
word in behalf of a class who are neither
thieves, prostitutes, nor Ragged School
scholars—who carry with them neither the
interesting excitement of crime, nor the
outward insignia of poverty ; whom few ever
hear of, and with whom fewer still ever
sympathise ?

My sympathy for them, and knowledge
of them, came by mere chance. Years ago,
at a large linen-draper's establishment where
I had long dealt, I noticed a flower which
one of the young women was wearing.

'Oh yes,' she said, with a sigh, 'it is very pretty'; adding, 'we very seldom see either a flower or a garden.' So, after thinking a little, I invited the young work-women to spend a Saturday afternoon in mine. This little outing became an annual festivity, looked forward to by myself as much as by them; so pleasant on both sides that my only wonder was how, out of the hundreds of customers of the shop who had houses and gardens, within easy distance of London, no one else ever thought of giving a similar invitation.

It would have cost very little money, and almost no trouble; for the mere sight and sound of country things and the delight of breathing country air was to my guests entertainment enough. Nor would it have offended the most refined household, since the girls did not come out of Hoxton, and were neither *Melendas* nor *Lizzies*—not at all the type of

workers whom Mr. Besant paints with such
vivid colours in his *Children of Gibeon*—
colours often supposed too terrible to be
true: but they are true, of a lower class of girls.

Between women who earn their bread by
their brains, such as authors, artists, governesses, etc., and those who gain a living by
manual labour—which, rightly or wrongly, is
considered 'menial'—there are many grades,
extending from the well-paid West End forewoman to the starving shirtmaker of the
East End. The upper ranks of this class,
which becomes every year more numerous
and more varied, are generally recruited
from the class above it; professional men's
daughters, who in the present justly high
standard of female education cannot be governesses—and will not be servants. For the
life of a dressmaker, milliner, or shop-girl
seems to them free, independent; above all
—what they most desire—not menial.

Therefore, at first with some surprise, I found among these my guests of successive years girls who could play, sing, and dance fully as well as your average 'young lady'; girls who could admire pictures and look longingly at full book-shelves; who enjoyed birds and flowers, and had evidently all the refined tastes which sharpen the sting of poverty, and make harder still the (burthen) of perpetual work. They often told me that they looked forward to this half-day's holiday for months, and talked about it for months afterwards. It was to them so much : while to me it gave the very smallest amount of thought and trouble. A dozen out of the hundreds of ladies who dealt at the shop—a large and well-known one—might have made the poor tired girls similarly happy once a month all the year round.

I name these facts because it was through one of these, whose pale faces, infinitesimal appetites, and keen enjoyment of the simplest pleasures had so touched me year by year, that I came to know of a House of Rest where she was spending her fortnight's holiday. She begged I might be written to about it, that I might make public to her hard-working sisters its many advantages.

It is unwise to take things on trust or at random, so I consulted an excellent woman from the neighbourhood—Babbacombe, near Torquay, Devon—who had had a friend there for many weeks, at the end of which she (the friend) declared that the House of Rest was 'like a little heaven below.' So, being in the impartial position of knowing nothing whatever about the place, nor a soul connected with it, I determined to go down and look at it, and judge for myself.

It was 'the first mild day of March,' as Wordsworth writes, urging his sister to 'put on with speed her woodland dress,' as we all

of us long to do—especially those who have
been pent up all winter in towns, with snow,
and fog and leaden skies. Even I, who,
thank Heaven, live in the country, felt my
heart dance as the train whirled me through
the rich Devon meadows between Exeter
and Torquay, with the sun shining on hillside
patches of lingering snow and low-lying fields
where the floods were still out. Birds were
singing wherever the train stopped at country
stations, and here and there the tiniest of young
lambs were tottering after their mothers. All
was rest, and peace, and promise of spring—
spring, which makes even the most conscientious worker long wildly for a holiday.

I had been rather hardworked too—
enough to make one recall what holidays
used to be when one was young and could
not get them—the insane craving for sunshine and fresh air, for green leaves and
primroses. And as the country grew lovelier

every minute, while the train dashed along,
and the fine sea-coast of Dawlish and Teign-
mouth appeared in glimpses between tunnels,
and through the open window came breaths
of Devon air—which is to East Anglian air
what cream is to double-skimmed milk—I
could have fancied myself a London shop-
girl, or telegraph clerk, or milliner's appren-
tice, taking my fortnight's holiday—fourteen
days out of 365!—and imagined what bliss it
would be to find a real House of Rest in this
beautiful corner of England.

The day after, I went to see it. Not in
sunshine, but pelting rain ; which obliterated
all the pretty road between Torquay and
Babbacombe, and blotted out the charming
view from the high point of land on which
the house stands, just over Oddicombe Bay
and sands. No matter. I could see inside
the house—and the ladies who started it,
who live close by, and overlook and guide

everything. They are two Misses Skinner (I am obliged to be personal : and I believe most good works originate not in a committee, but in a *person*), sisters, of moderate independent fortune, which, like many excellent single women, they expend upon others rather than themselves. One hot July day, about ten years since, these ladies, standing at the door of a shop in Edgeware Road, London, and noticing the pale and wearied faces inside, said to one another, 'I wish we could bring those poor girls down to our Babbacombe Beach !'

The wish was father not only to the thought, but the deed. Within a year they had laid all their plans, collected enough subscriptions to take a cottage with six beds, a little parlour and kitchen, and were ready to receive six shop-girls to spend their autumn holiday. Waiting for these (the hostesses being as nervous as the guests, or more so) they saw the Torquay Railway omnibus stop at the door, with five girls therein. They heard one say to the rest, 'Stay here till I see what it's like,' and then after a brief investigation return. 'You may get out. They're ladies—and the china's *thin;* so it isn't an Institution.'

If it had been, these poor tired holiday-makers afterwards declared, nothing would have induced them to enter it. They would have gone on and spent their small combined funds somewhere else, probably in ways far less advantageous and even reputable; for one can understand what a thronged seaside place in August is to a handful of young people who have been hard at work all the year—to whom, as one of them said to Miss Skinner, 'It's nothing but bed and business —business and bed—all year long.'

This little incident showed to the two benevolent ladies the lines upon which they must work if they wished to do any good by their scheme. They must avoid the appearance of its being a charity-scheme, with patrons, committee, secretaries, etc. Nor was it wholly a charity : the class for which it was chiefly meant could afford to pay something—and twelve shillings a week was settled as the maximum of what they should pay. Those who came recommended by subscribers (for subscriptions, quite necessary, were sought and found) were only asked five shillings a week ; and some, who could pay nothing at all, were paid for—nobody being any the wiser. It was decided that to keep up the girls' self-respect and soothe their sensitive pride—and the Misses Skinner soon found out that their inmates had plenty of both these qualities—no guest should be told how much another guest paid.

So they started—scarcely as a family ; that would have been an impossible fiction

—but as a sort of family boarding-house for working-women of the better class. And here ensued a difficulty. They had to draw the line somewhere, and, after long consideration, they did it, with a firm hand: excluding governesses on the one side, and domestic servants on the other. For this some critical friends blamed them; but, for my part, I think the Misses Skinner were right. A governess—if what a governess ought to be —would have little sympathy in common with shop-girls and needle-women; and, though many an individual domestic servant is superior to many a dressmaker, still, while the world lasts, these class-prejudices will exist, and it is foolish needlessly to fight against them, for they are founded on the common-sense law that though liberty and fraternity exist, and ought to exist in all ranks, equality is impossible. It is not in the nature of things.

Another rule—and a most righteous one
—these ladies made from the first in their
House of Rest, without which it would have
been unworthy of its name. Moral character
they held to be indispensable, but as to religious faith no questions were asked. The
girls were at liberty to attend any place of
worship they liked—or none. For, alas! it
was soon discovered that many of them went
to none. They were not heathens ; but their
week-day work was so incessant that they
generally spent half the Sunday in bed and
the other half in lolling about—at least those
who were ignorant. But many were not
ignorant, and these their hard and lonely
life had often turned into unbelievers. The
Misses Skinner gradually began to discover
that among their inmates were some—very
well educated and thoughtful—who openly
professed themselves Positivists, Agnostics,
even Atheists—if there is such a thing as a

real Atheist.   To drive these poor outsiders
into any regular pastoral fold would have
been madness—to turn them out would have
been cruelty.   Therefore these two excellent
Christian women decided that the wisest
thing was to leave them alone : to have daily
family prayers, which those could attend who
chose, but to make no religious duties com-
pulsory, and lead back these stray wanderers
by the silent influence and example of a
Christian household.   Proselytising in any
form, either by the Christians or non-
Christians, was absolutely forbidden.

Socially, the laws laid down were those
of ordinary society — cultured society — for
there were books, a piano, games ; everybody was expected to appear in the parlour
neatly dressed, and to conduct herself there
with good manners.   What lay underneath,
in each individual, no other individual could
tell ; but a general sympathetic supervision—

without obnoxious surveillance—was generally able soon to guess at, and act accordingly ; for the Misses Skinner have, though
a gentle, a very firm hand in holding the
reins of government.

Thus they began, making as few rules as
possible, but keeping steadily to those they
did make.   Their girls gathered about them.
In 1880 they were able to take a house with
fifteen beds instead of five ; the year after
twenty-nine beds found continual occupants ;
and last year, 1886, the house—a good-sized
ordinary residence near to their own—was so
full that they required all summer to take
twenty beds outside in Babbacombe village.
Now, a still larger house close by has fallen
empty, and, if their funds permit, instead of six
they will be able to accommodate sixty girls,
in time for the yearly holidays after the
London season is over.   July, August, and
September are the months when these sort

of workers come ; but telegraph clerks, of whom there are many, have their holidays chiefly in the winter, so that the House of Rest is never empty.

'And now let us go across and see it,' said, after these explanations, the younger Miss Skinner, who chiefly does the talking and writing and bookkeeping; while her sister, aided by a matron and two servants, attends to all the domestic affairs. These two ladies and a third volunteer — Miss Roberts, of Torquay, well known as the author of *Mademoiselle Mori* — make up the entire committee; and any one who knows what committees are, especially ladies' committees, will say 'So best.'

Through a neat entrance - hall, adorned with plants, we passed to a drawing-room— really a drawing-room — with a piano, and books, and engravings on the walls, and 'pretty things' all scattered about; as pleasant a room as one could wish to sit in on a wet day. Its inmates, women of various ages, neatly dressed, and each busy about something or other, welcomed us with smiling courtesy.

'It is one of the rules of the house,' Miss Skinner told me afterwards, 'that everybody should show to new-comers or accidental visitors the same politeness she would think necessary in a house of her own.'

Some of these girls looked healthy and bright, others sickly and sad; but all were ready to talk and be pleasant. I noticed that they were all addressed as '*Miss* So-and-so,' except when, as not seldom happened, one of the ladies called them 'dear,' at which their faces always brightened up. The sweet word was not thrown away— loving - kindness never is. How many a forlorn worker may have had her heart warmed and strengthened by the motherly tenderness found in this House of Rest!

Its interior and invisible arrangements
were equal to the visible. The bedrooms
when small had only one bed—at most two ;
but the larger ones were subdivided into four
by the simple device of two iron bars crossing in the centre, upon which curtains run—
thus secluding safely éach little bed, wash-
stand, table, and box for clothes. Every
room was painted a different colour, and
called thence 'the peacock room,' 'the blue
room,' 'the pink room.' The earthenware
was also varied and pretty ; in short, every
pains was taken to make the House of Rest
as little as possible like a House of Deten-
tion or House of Correction, which many
such practically are.

'Will you be surprised to learn,' said Miss
Skinner, with a smile, 'that we not only
allow, we actually encourage dancing, singing, and acting of charades ? We give pic-
nics on the sands, or send our girls boating,

with a boatman we can trust. Nay, we even permit excursions up the Dart, and to many other of the lovely places hereabouts. Our guests generally club together and pay their own expenses ; if they cannot, we sometimes pay. But not often ; for there is in most of them a stern, even fierce independence, equal to that of Mr. Besant's *Melenda*. The world has. dealt so hardly with them that they have grown bitter. They cannot understand how anybody means to be kind to them — above all, why my sister and I should do so much for them, when we get nothing by it.'

Is not this the very lesson that our democratic age requires—the personal help, the personal sympathy between rich and poor, which does more good than any amount of money ?

I inquired which class of female workers she considered the 'best off,' in all senses.

'Decidedly the telegraph and post-office clerks. They are better educated, to begin with, and more healthy, both because their work is healthier, and because the rooms they work in have, thanks to Mr. Fawcett, all sanitary appliances. His interest in them and his care over them ended but with his life. But with the West-End, and especially the East-End shopkeepers, it is very different. I could tell you things my girls have told me that would wring your heart.'

But she did not, and does not, tell—which accounts for the girls' confidence in her. Only by urging the usefulness of my purpose, for which an ounce of fact was worth a cart-load of fiction, did she give me, anonymously, some out of many data—notes made by herself at the time—proving that Mr. Besant has not overdrawn his picture, as so many are inclined to think. I set the cases down, unembellished and nameless.

'A——, mantle-maker in a large establishment. Wages 9s. per week, latterly only
7s. 6d., work being slack. Pays 3s. 6d. for
room, 1s. for coal, lamp-oil, and firewood,
9d. for washing, which leaves just 3s. 9d. for
food and clothing. Lives mostly on bread
and tea; carries bread and butter for her
dinner to her place of business, as it takes
her three hours to walk there and back. A
kind forewoman paid for her coming to the
House of Rest. She is a pretty, graceful
girl of twenty. She said once, with a sigh,
"It is *so* hard to keep respectable!" One of
the plush mantles she made was for the
Princess of Wales, value £30.' (Good
heavens! if that sweet, gentle Princess, the
mother of young daughters, had known this
history when she put it on!)

'B—— is a bodice hand. After five
years' experience earns 8s. a week. Says
simply, "Often I don't get quite enough to

eat." Has no parents; boards with a step-mother. Her sister earns only 6s. 6d. a week. They have hard work to get decent clothes; and the town they live in, a gay watering - place, makes it difficult to keep respectable.'

'C—— was a girl strongly like *Melenda*, pale and fierce-looking. She had been long out of work with pleurisy and an injured limb. Lives mostly on tea. When quite well (if ever) she rises at 5.30 A.M., and goes to bed at midnight. She too is an orphan, alone in the world.'

'We gave her drives — she could not walk,' Miss Skinner added; 'and you never saw anything like her delight in country things.'

'D——, a mantle-cutter. Cloth so heavy to lift that she strained her back, result being acute neuralgia of the spine. She had an invalid sister to support, and her regular work only lasts through eight months of the year.'

Ordinarily, neither sick people nor convalescents are taken at the House of Rest, which is meant for a holiday-house, to prevent illness, not cure it. But sometimes invalids come threatened with that almost universal scourge, consumption. 'We all of us have something more or less wrong with our lungs,' said one girl. And no wonder. In a house, which is one of the largest establishments in London, the workroom is only lighted by a skylight, bitterly cold in winter, 'baking hot' in summer. Sixty women work in it, and it is warmed by one small stove. Another, a provincial workroom, where fifteen sit daily, has no means of fire at all. When cold, they light the gas, and there is no ventilation of any sort. But to continue.

Case after case might be set down, with the girls' own simple words to illustrate it.

'All trees, and birds singing, and *no people !*'
exclaimed in delight one who had spent her
life in the East End of London, and never
had a country holiday before.   'In eleven
months and a fortnight I will be back again,'
said another, 'and I'll put by a penny a week
for going up the Dart.'   This girl, a book-
binder, with parents to keep, would after all
have lost her holiday, for she spent all the
money laid up for it over her sick father, had
not a kind lady given her the sum required,
and she came.

E—— and F—— were worse off than
she.   E—— had never had a holiday, except
for three days, in her whole life, and seemed
absolutely stupefied with work.   F—— had
stood in a shop for six years without rest, and
had never seen the sea before.   She was a
girl with little or no education, yet had set
her face as a flint against much immorality
that she saw around her in the said shop, and

held to the right with a marvellous stead-
fastness.

This is the great terror haunting these
poor girls, who as a class are 'respectable,'
and desire to keep so. There are worse
things before them than mere dying.

Of the thousand women who in ten years
have visited the House of Rest, and whose
after career has been, as usual, silently
watched by their friends there, many, only
too many, have died ; but only one has, to
use the customary and most pathetic word,
' fallen.'

To keep them safe from falling, to give
them innocent pleasures for guilty ones—
young people must have pleasure, in some
form or other—to offer them a higher ideal
of life, wholesome interests, and cheerful
companionships, which often ripen into bene-
ficial friendships, is the aim of the Babbacombe
House of Rest. It does not profess to cure

the sick, or reclaim the wicked; it goes on
the principle that 'prevention is better than
cure,' and that to guide people into the right
way is safer and more efficacious than to
snatch them out of the wrong one.

It is meant principally as a holiday-home,
small enough to allow its promoters individual
knowledge of the inmates. They find out
what each likes best, and help her to it, so
that she may go back to work strengthened
and refreshed.

The more so, as this yearly holiday is to
many girls their most dangerous time. Having saved up for it throughout the year, they
are bent on enjoying it to the full while it
lasts. They spend their money, often very
recklessly; make acquaintances not always
creditable; and this brief taste of the life of
enjoyment makes more intolerable than ever
the life of work. They loathe it, and see
ever before them the one ghastly means of

escaping from it which the world offers to its starving surplus women. If the happy women, fulfilling their natural duties as wives and mothers, and the not unhappy single women, who have found their work and do it, and whose influence often radiates far wider than that of any married woman, would only try to help their sisters *before* they fall!

There are many ways of doing this. First, by only dealing at shops where they know the employées are well treated, as in many cases they are: notably at Marshall and Snelgrove's, Waterloo House (now joined to Swan and Edgar's), Gorringe's, Debenham and Freebody's, Lewis and Allenby's, Harvey Nichols', and Redmayne's. Out of London, and in the provinces, where the discomfort and disregard of all sanitary care is much worse than in the metropolis, there are still many admirable exceptions—

such as Walter Cobb, of Sydenham ; Tucker and Son, of Exeter ; Jolly and Sons, of Bath. Of all these firms, Miss Skinner informed us, their young people who have been at the House of Rest speak in the highest terms.

A second form of help is the very simple one I named at the beginning of this paper —that any lady who gives garden-parties should give just one a year to guests who cannot return it, but who will enjoy it to an extent she can hardly imagine. And thirdly, that any other lady who is anxious to do good, but really does not know how to do it —since to go and live for three months at Hoxton, after the fashion of Mr. Besant's heroine, would only be possible in fiction— may assist others to do good by communicating with the Misses Skinner at Babbacombe.

I wish I could draw a picture of the House of Rest as I saw it next morning—a

thorough spring morning — sitting on the
cliff-top, with the sunshiny sea glittering at
my feet, and the curve of coast, with its
various *combes*, or valleys—Oddicombe, Wat-
combe, Maidencombe, Holcombe — visible
almost to Portland, with the rich colouring
for which Devonshire is famous, the dark red
earth contrasting with the green vegetation.
Then the delicious air, soft, yet bracing ; for
Babbacombe is higher and fresher than
Torquay, and healthy all the year round. I
thought of the poor pale girls (both the well-
to-do, who can pay for themselves, and those
who cannot pay—though no one here knows
which is which except the Misses Skinner)
coming down from London workrooms,
bathing, boating (the sands lie just below),
making day excursions ; taking long walks
through the lovely Devon lanes ; having
innocent, merry companionship among themselves—no strict rules, beyond those of an

ordinary civilised household—no preaching, no proselyting—no attempt to 'do their souls good,' except by placing before them the beauty of daily Christian life. And I felt glad and thankful to know that such things exist still, and that it is really possible for a small handful of good women to have started and kept up what is truly 'a little heaven below,' in this bad and troublesome world.

THE STORY OF AN OLD FRIEND

EVERYBODY knows the Crystal Palace. Not only Great Britain, but the whole of the civilised and semi-civilised world, has contributed its quota to the sixty millions who, during the last thirty-three years, have been amused, delighted, and educated — for an education truly it is—under that great glass roof at Sydenham, whose familiar glimmer shines in the sunlight to all the country round. And yet, in a sense, almost nobody knows it; its history, its resources, its endless nooks and corners, where not merely days but weeks might be spent in examining treasures unnoticed by the general public; its library, sculpture and picture galleries, architectural reproductions, museums, and, above all, its music, the perfection of which, as a whole, is absolutely unequalled. What capital in Europe has furnished the same amount of admirable performances as those given season after season on successive Saturdays, ever since 1855? And where have there been—where could there be—Handel Festivals like those which have taken place here triennially for the last thirty years?

It may not be inappropriate, now that some people say our old friend on the hill-top is *in articulo mortis*—and, indeed, it is an open secret that the Crystal Palace is, financially, in a critical condition—if in its despondent age some facts are recapitulated of its hopeful youth and all the good aims which it has carried out so successfully, to the content of all the world—except the shareholders.

A whole generation has gone by since that June day in 1854, when the Queen, still a young Queen, stood with her young husband at her side, amidst a brilliant crowd —of which the few that yet survive and still remember it are old and gray—to open the new Crystal Palace at Sydenham. What she said, in answer to the 'loyal and dutiful address,' has been so long forgotten, that it may well be printed as historical.

'It is a source of the highest gratification to myself and to the Prince, my Consort, to find that the Great Exhibition of 1851, which was so happily inaugurated under our auspices, suggested the idea of this magnificent undertaking, which has produced so noble a monument of the genius, science, and enterprise of my subjects. It is my earnest wish and hope that the bright anticipations which have been formed as to its future destiny may, under the blessing of Divine Provi-

dence, be completely realised, and that the
wonderful structure, and the treasures of
art and knowledge it contains, may long
continue to elevate and instruct, as well as
to delight and amuse, the minds of all classes
of my people.'

In these last two lines Her Majesty con-
densed the aim of the founders of the Crystal
Palace—not only to 'delight and amuse,' but
to 'elevate and instruct.' She had need to
speak warmly of 'that enterprise.' When,
in 1852, Government declined to purchase
the building in Hyde Park which had con-
stituted the first Great Exhibition, nine
gentlemen stepped in to save the beautiful
fabric from annihilation. Their names—
deserving of record—were, T. N. Farquhar,
Francis Fuller, Robert Gill, Harman Grise-
wood, Joseph Leech, J. C. Morice, Scott
Russell, Leo Schuster, and Samuel Laing.
They formed themselves into a Company,

of which Mr., now Sir George, Grove was the Secretary ; bought a site of three hundred acres at Sydenham, and removed there, re-erected in more than its pristine beauty the fairy Palace, which for a whole summer had been the centre of what was then called 'the World's Fair.' Besides the sympathising public, with its purse in its hand, they were aided by men of science and general capacity in every branch of art. Owen Jones and Digby Wyatt, Joseph Bonomi, Professors Owen, Ansted, and Edward Forbes, with many others, most of whom have now passed away from among us, gave valuable and hearty help. Sir Joseph Paxton, who from being the Duke of Devonshire's gardener at Chatsworth, rose to world-wide notoriety, was the soul of it all.

No labour or expense was spared to make the Palace a medium of instruction in everything that can be taught through the eye. The sculpture gallery alone—consisting of casts from all the finest antiques in Europe —cost £40,000. Palms and other rare trees, which for a whole century had been collected by Messrs. Loddige of Hackney, were purchased by Sir Joseph Paxton for internal decoration ; while externally the natural advantages of the site lent themselves to his landscape gardening, as unique as it was beautiful. Without, the geology of the ancient world, with its strange extinct animals of a prehistoric period, was made patent to the commonest eye by the ingenuity of various modellers, guided by Professor Owen ; while, within the building, the Ethnological Department, under Mr. Waterhouse and Mr. Gould, illustrated the different races throughout the globe by curious groups of the genus *homo* in various stages of civilisation. Mr. Fergusson and

Mr. Layard aided in the arrangement of the
Assyrian, and Owen Jones of the Egyptian
Courts. From Carnac, Philæ, Beni Hassan,
were brought reproductions of the wonders
of the old Eastern world, refined and civilised when we Westerns were still barbarians
of the lowest type. Some of us may yet
remember how we stood and gazed in
wonder at the two gigantic statues from
the tomb of Abou Simbel, and how in the
great fire which twenty-one years ago destroyed the tropical department, these grand
figures were seen sitting solemn with their
hands on their knees, the flames playing
about them, until at last they sank slowly
into the mass of fiery ruin.

Sir Joseph Paxton was the designer of
the fountains, familiar to us all, and said to
be the largest artificial fountains in the world.
They rise, in their central columns, to the
height of 280 feet, and a grand display

consumes 6,000,000 gallons of water. It
is drawn from an Artesian well in the
grounds, which, well and bore together,
pierces to a depth of 575 feet. Thence
the water rises to the top of the two water
towers, planned by the late Mr. Brunel,
constructed of cast-iron upon an enormously
solid foundation—a triumph of engineering
skill as well as economy. The water is conveyed to and from the reservoirs in pipes,
of which the weight is reckoned at 4000
tons, and the total length 10 miles.

These statistics, now almost forgotten,
for the work is done and most of the
workers dead, show on what a grand scale,
and with what careful prevision, the Crystal
Palace was first built. Naturally, being
made of more perishable materials than
most buildings, it has required constant
supervision and repair; yet after more than
thirty years even the skeleton of its structure

shows little sign of age; the iron pillars are as light and firm, and the great glass roof shines as bright as when it first rose up in Hyde Park, a kind of Aladdin's palace, the delight and wonder of all eyes. We have ceased to wonder now, being so familiar with it; we have all but forgotten the very name of Sir Joseph Paxton, the fine old man whose bust still stands on the terrace, looking out on the gardens he planned, with his wonderful Palace glittering behind him. But he did his work, and nobly it was done.

The Crystal Palace was fairly started; but probably none of the projectors contemplated the various directions in which it would soon ramify. One point they seem completely to have overlooked—music. No special music-room had been provided; that devoted to musical instruments, afterwards known as the Bohemian Glass Court, was all there was to play in. The Directors thought that light

military tunes would alone suit the taste of
the Crystal Palace visitors. But fate decided
differently.

In its small occasional band, by no means
a regular orchestra, was a German piccolo
player, by name August Manns. This young
man, in whom the Secretary had the acute-
ness to detect not only great musical genius,
but a power of musical organisation, subse-
quently developed to an extent now uni-
versally recognised, was appointed Musical
Director. Immediately he set about his
work. Out of the sixty-four wind-instru-
ments he selected thirty-four ; added to them
four professional ' strings,' and with this improvised ' scratch ' orchestra—himself playing
the solo violin—he began, on October 20,
1856, the first of those Saturday Concerts
which have delighted and instructed the
musical public to an extent which can hardly
be over-appreciated.

Within two months the Musical Instruments Court was found much too small for his audience, and Mr. Manns had to utilise the South Transept, and afterwards a lecture-room. Besides the Saturdays, daily concerts of an hour each were given. Continual practice together improved the executants as much as the taste of the audience. In music, as in most things, a conductor must either guide or follow his public. Mr. Manns wisely chose to do the former. In a letter written lately, reverting to those old days, he himself says, and it is worth repeating: ' By means of our daily performances the question as to what class of compositions should be principally brought before the people on whose patronage the Crystal Palace depended, was practically tested. The necessity of providing for the daily concerts throughout the year music which should please the varied tastes of the multitude, convinced me of the grand fact that the best works of the best masters contain the largest amount of that soul-life of musical art which touches the hearts not only of the cultured but the uncultured, most surely, quickly, and lastingly.'

Working on this basis, with the aid of the Secretary, but not always of the Directors, Mr. Manns during that first season succeeded in giving to a steadily-increasing audience three Beethoven symphonies, Mendelssohn's violin symphony, and many classical fragments, besides a Mozart Celebration, which was warmly approved.

Some of us old folks may still call to mind that newly-collected orchestra, consisting mostly of young performers, with its energetic young conductor. What a picture he was! slender and wiry, with his long hair flying, and his white-gloved hands gesticulating wildly, especially during rehearsals, when he poured himself out in impassioned German, or still more impetuous broken English, explaining, encouraging, sometimes storming—but always with the pardonable passion of a man thoroughly in earnest, who thinks not of himself but of his Art. August Manns—decidedly a 'character'—got to be known at the Crystal Palace, as well as the 'G.,' recognised by everybody as George Grove, who wrote for the programmes such admirable critical essays, full of the most interesting musical facts and analyses.

Despite the coldness of unmusical officials, he and the Musical Director held their own. The orchestra, warmed into equal enthusiasm, improved monthly and yearly. Though German himself, and no doubt believing in his own countrymen, as we are all rather prone to do, Mr. Manns conscientiously Anglicised his band to a very great extent.

Sixteen to thirty-six was the proportion of Germans to English at starting, and it is still much the same : in one year only the proportion being twenty-one to fifty-one. French, Italians, Poles, and Swedes count by units only ; evidently Mr. Manns's chief reliance has been upon English and German executants.   The total number of his regular orchestra has been from fifty-five, where it stood for five consecutive years, to eighty-three, where it stands now.   Not counting, of course, any extra aid required for extra performances.   It would be difficult to find a body of musicians, and a head, who have done for so many years such good and con-tinuous service to Art.   For, it must be remembered, they play every day, sometimes twice a day, besides the Saturday winter and famous opera concerts—and they *never* play 'rubbish'; indeed, some of the music in their *repertoire* is as difficult as any ever written.

Not till 1859 did they find a permanent *locale* in the present Concert-room, where, Saturday after Saturday was gathered a steadily-increasing audience, silent, attentive; listening with more and more appreciation to the highest form of recognised classical music, as well as to the then unrecognised 'music of the future'— at first, to their amazement, then their perplexity, and finally to their universal delight. Nothing is more confirmatory of the fact that the masses can be educated into the love of really good music, than to look round at a Crystal Palace concert and see the eager, intent faces—a large proportion reading from their scores; and notice also the total silence, no chattering, no laughing, and the uncontrolled burst of applause when anything specially pleases. Moreover—what is not always the case at concerts—they generally applaud the right things; for claptrap, com-

monplace, or feeble sentimentalism is toler-
ated neither by Mr. Manns nor his
audience.

But this is what the Crystal Palace has
now grown to; and we are recording its
beginnings. All great movements are generally the work of some energetic individual
—and August Manns happened to be that
individual. His Saturday Concerts established themselves in public favour; and
presently musicians began to think of
travelling farther.

The bicentenary of Handel's death suggested a memorial celebration worthy of the
great English composer — for English he
truly was, in all but the accident of birth;
and the large auditorium of the Crystal
Palace seemed a fitting place for it. The
improvised orchestra in the Central Transept on the opening day had produced effects
that gave every hope of success as regarded

acoustics; and the summer grace and beauty of the Palace outdid any London concert-room in airiness, comfort, and pleasantness.

Nevertheless, when a preliminary Festival was organised by the Sacred Harmonic Society in June 1857, there were not wanting those who foreboded no end of misfortunes, among the rest that the yet untried reverberation of such a body of sound would cause the glass of the roof to crack and fall down upon the heads of the unfortunate audience! However, Rehearsal Day came —and nothing happened. On June 15, the attendance had risen from 5844 to 11,159. On June 17 the Queen and the Prince Consort drove down from Buckingham Palace to hear the rarely-performed *Judas Maccabæus;* and on June 19 an audience of 17,000 listened to the marvellous *Israel in Egypt,* given as it never had been given before, and as it never could be heard any-

where but in the Crystal Palace. Two
thousand voices, selected from London and
the provinces, formed the chorus; the
orchestra numbered nearly 600, and among
the soloists were Madame Clara Novello
(who that heard her 'I know that my Re-
deemer liveth' will ever forget it?), Madame
Rudersdorff, Miss Dolby, Mr. Weiss, Herr
Formes, etc. Among the list Mr. Sims
Reeves is the only noted singer still before
the public; nearly all the rest, with their
conductor, Michael Costa, have passed 'into
the Silent Land.'

That a Handel Festival thus organised
would be perfectly successful was now
proved; and for two years Mr. Costa, Mr.
Manns, and Mr. George Grove worked un-
tiringly to that end—with the natural result.
The great festival of 1859 fulfilled their
every hope, both artistically and practically;
proving, as the *Times* averred in its critique,

'a singular example of what private enterprise and energy, unbacked by Government
aid, is able to accomplish in a free land and
under a constitutional *régime.*' It also
proved that our unmusical England was
capable of musical efforts which in grandeur,
in unanimity, and in the conscientious, unselfish working together of large masses of
executants for one great end, threw all other
countries into the shade. Meyerbeer, who
was present, declared that, after his lifelong
experience of European musical solemnities,
he thought this *Israel in Egypt*, at the
Crystal Palace, surpassed them all.

It does so still. A musician who remembers all the Festivals, from the overwhelming
effect of the opening burst of 'God save the
Queen' at the first one, down to the final
chords of 'The Horse and his Rider hath He
thrown into the Sea' (it is impossible to write
in words the notes which music-lovers know

so well) in June 1885, can imagine nothing
on this side heaven more like heaven, more
completely realising the idea of 'that great
multitude which no man can number,' than
this mass of melodious sound; invisible, in-
tangible, and yet so overwhelming—the only
mortal delight which is absolutely and entirely
spiritual.

Seven triennial Festivals were held, with
undiminished success, the Sacred Harmonic
Society taking the musical arrangements, and
the Crystal Palace Company doing all the
rest.   For the eighth Festival, 1883, the
Sacred Harmonic being ended, the Crystal
Palace Company took all arrangements into
its own hands, with Sir Michael Costa still
as conductor, and a body of 4000 chorus-
singers and 500 instrumentalists, all volun- .
tary, to follow his baton.   There was also a
new organ — Handel's Organ Concertos,
played by Mr. W. T. Best, having become

a great feature of Selection Day. A huge velarium overhead and canvas wings at the side had been erected to confine the enormous body of sound a little, and give to the soloists less fatigue in singing, and better chance of being heard at a distance.

As usual, the giant orchestra did its work perfectly, and an auditory of unprecedented number listened with delight. Costa outdid himself, and no one present could forget the ringing cheers of welcome and adieu to the conductor from both performers and audience, unconscious that it was for the last time.

Two years after, when another exceptional Handel Festival was planned, Sir Michael was too ill to undertake it; and the vacant conductorship was offered to Mr. Manns. Not without many doubts—which the first rehearsal dispelled. By the opening day of the Festival it was clearly seen that Mr.

I

Manns was as capable of managing 5000 executants as 50.

The choruses in the *Messiah* went marvellously, and the *Israel* — with its gigantic effects carried out as under no other circumstances could be possible — was a triumph of musical sublimity. The next Handel Festival—and another one is due in 1888— promises to be even finer—if there is still a Crystal Palace to hold it in.

'Ay, that's the rub!' With all its outward charms and successes, its solid internal usefulnesses, our old friend does not pay. It is difficult to account for this. Some urge the distance from London—yet the huge southern outskirts of the metropolis ought to furnish a public of their own. Others say that the continual repairs required in such fragile materials eat away profits, as well as the enormous expenses attendant upon the effort to combine a People's Palace of amusement

with an educational establishment for Science
and Art. Thus, 'between two stools'—so
proverbially true!—the Palace falls to the
ground.

Shall it fall? Cannot something be done
either by Government aid, or, far better, by
private effort, to tide the Directors over
these quicksands into smooth water? Does
the nation understand what it would lose
were the Crystal Palace to be swept away?
and how much both upper and lower, *i.e.*
educated and uneducated, classes are interested in its preservation?

First, the former. Nowhere in England
is there such a fine collection of casts from
foreign antiques, many of them the only
casts ever taken, and of curious mediæval
monuments, artistic and architectural. Some
of these—spread about the dim and seldom-
visited side courts—would repay an artist for
weeks of study. Then there is the School

of Art, Science, and Literature, now in its twenty-seventh session, each session having counted, at fewest, 500 students. During the past fifteen years no less than 9000 students, guided by thirty-three instructors, have attended the classes. The School of Practical Engineering — established in the grounds in 1872—has educated 900 young men, and is still advancing; paying its own way, and giving complete satisfaction. There is also under the charge of Mr. F. K. T. Shenton, one of the ablest and most devoted of those to whom the Crystal Palace owes its origin and continued existence, a Reading-room, a library for reference, and lending, under certain restrictions; Oxford and Cambridge local examinations, and daily classes of all sorts—from the higher education of women, down (or up?) to cookery and dancing. All these educational institutions are worked at a money profit, and do

not cost the Company anything; while the
Art and Science collections, thus utilised,
are in some sort an endowment. Finally,
where can the true musician, be he professional or amateur, find such music—not only
on Saturdays, but every day and all the year
round—as he finds at the Crystal Palace?

Such are its advantages to the cultivated
classes: now as to those to whom cultivation
must be given, as we give it to little children,
through the vehicle of amusement. Nothing
educates the British artisan—the very back-
bone of the community—nothing keeps him
out of discontent, and consequently mischief,
like a wholesome holiday. And nowhere do
you see him at better advantage than when
he spends his holiday at Sydenham. The
annual Temperance Fête,—where I have
seen over 50,000 persons enjoying themselves without a drop of that accursed alcohol
which is the cause of half the crime and

misery of our three kingdoms,—the Tonic
Sol-Fa, the Foresters and Police Festivals,
are refreshing to witness; and very seldom
is there, even on Bank Holidays, anything
that what we call 'a lady' would dislike to
witness, if she be a woman who loves to see
her fellow-creatures happy.

During this exceptionally fine summer,
when for two months the graceful, classical,
altogether unobjectionable ballet of the
'Sculptor's Dream' has been played in the
open air night after night, a more innocently
happy crowd could hardly be found than that
which throngs the terraces and gardens till
10.30 P.M.; parents with their children,
groups of friends and pairs of sweethearts,
with apparently nothing of that evil element
which it is so difficult to keep out of pro-
miscuous public gatherings:—the social
'pitch,' of which the least touch defiles.
That the Directors and officials may con-

tinue to keep it out, and yet provide the honest and most desirable amusement which the Crystal Palace can offer to the working classes, is much to be desired.

But this will need care. The Company must take pains to furnish both mental and the not-to-be despised bodily food, of a really wholesome kind. And in some things the anxiety of the Directors to make and save money has led them to lower the public taste by giving painfully puerile entertainments, and pantomimes coarser than even the coarsenesses of London theatres. Why should it be so ? Why not make the pretty little theatre, where since 1870 innumerable plays and operas, bad, good, and indifferent, have been given, a vehicle for giving the enormous suburban public, which cannot go to London for its dramatic entertainments, a chance of seeing there the best of everything, and *only the best* ? If this were

wisely done, surely the innumerable families
who populate the outskirts of London would
throng to such performances; where an
afternoon's pleasure may be gained at half
the cost and trouble of going to London
theatres, and coming back worn and jaded in
the middle of the night.

Another want—very necessary and very
ill-supplied—the Directors would do well to
investigate. In a 'day out' creature-com-
forts must be considered. The honest
British workman, his wife and family, the
country cousins, the work-girl and her
'young man,' do not require grand dinners—
doubtless well supplied here; but they do
want 'something to eat'—and drink; a cup
of really good tea or coffee, tolerable bread,
butter, cold meat—perhaps even a glass of
beer, though of that most unrefreshing
'refreshment' the less said the better. After
going about the Palace and grounds all day

they need a good meal, at once wholesome and inexpensive, and—they do not get it. They get only a rough 'feed,' not 'cheap,' and decidedly 'nasty.' The Aerated Bread Company—which has now its shops throughout London, where for the sum of twopence you can get a cup of admirable tea or coffee, and for sevenpence can make a hearty and excellent meal, served on neat clean tables, by active and civil waitresses, not waiters—would at the Crystal Palace be an indescribable boon.

So perhaps would two or three intelligent guides, who for a small fee might conduct the ignorant visitors to the various courts, and explain the objects of art, or the curiosities of science, which lie hidden there in corners where no one ever thinks of going. For there are numbers of the young generation—clerks, artisans, even day-labourers, hard-handed, but clear-headed—who

crave for education, and seek it eagerly in
the few ways open to them.   Such a place
as the Crystal Palace helps to smooth and
broaden the road—the right road—which
leads them upwards, not downwards, as so
many roads do.

It is essentially a People's Palace, and the
people must be amused as well as instructed.
Bicycling and gymnastics in summer and
skating in winter are attractions that should
never be overlooked or discontinued.   Illu-
minated promenades inside—and those who
have walked up and down the nave to the
sound of the great organ know what a
pretty sight this is—and green, winding
walks outside, in daylight or moonlight, will
do 'our poorer brethren' as much good as
the brilliant Handel Festivals do to the
upper classes, and are pleasures to which
they have an equal right.   For, desirable as
the half-crown Saturdays and the guinea

season tickets may be, the shilling days and
fête days, with their multitudinous throng of
merry, wondering visitors, are what the
Crystal Palace was really made for, and
should never be forgotten.

But there is one delight in which all sorts
and conditions of men, with their women
and children, can share; and it is a great
delight. He must be a very solid—I was
going to say 'stupid' individual who does
not enjoy fireworks! and the Crystal Palace
fireworks are absolutely unique of their kind.
But of the tens of thousands—sometimes as
many as twenty thousand a night—who go
to see them, probably not a dozen people
know anything more about them than is
beheld by the eye—though that is a great
deal. The armies of rockets fighting in the
sky, the Niagara of fire which comes pouring
over, the brilliant effects of light on the
fountains and trees, and the dazzling stars of

all colours which, bursting high up in the air, float slowly down, and vanish harmlessly before they touch the ground—nothing more beautiful in the pyrotechnic line can be conceived.

Does it occur to any one how all this has come about ? Some years ago a member of the Company's staff, Dr. David S. Price, Analytical Chemist in the Technological Department, discovered in a small back street the workshop of an almost unknown firework-maker named Brock. The two laid their heads together—and very clever heads they must have been !—the chemical knowledge of the one being added to the practical skill of the other. Every year new discoveries and ingenious combinations were made. The Crystal Palace Directors had the sense to see, as in the case of August Manns, that superior genius sometimes 'pays,' and they did not grudge the large sums that required to be expended. The result was that, even with their great costliness, calculated often at ten pounds per minute, the fireworks are remunerative; and they are the most splendid specimens of pyrotechnic art to be seen in all Europe.

.   But I must bring this history of our old friend to an end; unto which, people say, itself is shortly coming.   Must it come, after a beautiful and useful existence of more than thirty-three years?   After having provided pleasure and profit to a whole generation, and work to hundreds and thousands?   For the staff of officials it employs, within and without the building, is very great, and the amount of money which it has distributed in weekly salaries throughout the neighbourhood—a neighbourhood which it has itself created—must be beyond calculation.   Is all this to cease?   is the Palace to be swept away, its grounds to be turned into building land, and the suburb which has grown up around it to depreciate in value accordingly? Is London to miss that pleasant breathing-place, almost as good as the 'real country,' with its splendid view over miles of Kent? And must that enormous suburb south of the Thames lose its centre of attraction, which draws pleasure-seekers, and consequently money, by a network of railways from every part of the kingdom? Would not such a loss be acutely felt, even in a business point of view?

Some may say, it is too late—but nothing is too late for the energy of the British speculator. If a sufficient number of men could be found, who would combine business-like prudence and practical common sense with a 'soul above buttons'—a certain high-mindedness, which, while not objecting to make money, yet recognises that money should be made in a noble rather than an ignoble way—then we might hope that our old friend should renew his youth, and become all that we could desire.

Surely it cannot be too late! Let us all join practically in the fine old Cornish song—

> And shall our old friend die?
> And shall our old friend die?

Or twenty thousand Englishmen will know the reason why!

WORK FOR IDLE HANDS

FORTY years ago John Bright said, and would probably confirm his words now, 'The greatest cause of Ireland's calamities is that Ireland is idle! Ireland is idle, therefore she starves. Ireland starves, therefore she rebels. We must choose between industry and anarchy. But the idleness of the people of Ireland is not wholly their own fault; it is for the most part a forced idleness.'

How it began, and what caused it, I do not attempt to discuss here. Perhaps all discussion on the subject is a mistake. We must accept things as they are. When a house is in flames you do not begin to investigate the origin of the fire—you try to put it out. God knows whether anything will avert the total ruin of 'that most distressful country' which has possibilities of being one of the finest countries under the sun ; but everything ought to be tried. And I am going to relate an experiment which has been tried, and succeeded—of finding work for idle hands and putting bread into starving mouths for three years past: an experiment not political, but social, and conducted by 'only a woman.' Yet women have been at the root of half the revolutions of the world. And I believe, if Irish women would take 'Home Rule' into their own hands, and teach their sons, husbands, brothers, and lovers that, instead of fighting for one's rights, it is best to do one's duties—the first duty being *to work*—we should soon see light through the darkness of this, the darkest time that poor Ireland has ever known.

K

Yet it must be confessed that the faculty of work—plodding, persistent work—is not ingrained in the Celtic nature as it is in that of the Saxon and the Lowland Scot. The Irishman, like the Highlander, is capable of magnificent accidental effort, but he dislikes continuous toil. The power of finding out, or making his own work, and then sticking to it until it is done, is not in him as it is in the less imaginative and more phlegmatic races. Also—though this is a poor excuse, yet it ought to be considered — there is something in the moist, mild, rainy climate of the Green Isle which superinduces laziness. 'I never can work thoroughly unless I am out of Ireland,' said to me one of the most energetic young Irishmen I have ever known. Therefore, in endorsing John Bright's theory, we have to take the Irish nation as they are, and not expect from them qualities belonging to other nations, subject to the climatic influences of other lands. Doubtless a different race—Teuton, Norse, or even the steady young Saxon — would have reclaimed the many thousand acres of bogland in the centre of Ireland, or of moor and mountain land round her coasts; would have fished her plentiful seas and rivers, and planted manufactures in her decaying towns. But all this needs capital; and where is it? Still, as a proof of what a moderate sum can effect when wisely used — Ireland and the Irish being dealt with as they are, and not as they might have been—I wish to tell a simple story.

In the Inventions Exhibition many must have noted a stall devoted to Irish Cottage Industries, of which the work was beautiful enough to receive a special commendation. It had originated thus: In the summer of 1883 Mrs. Ernest Hart, an English lady, with her husband, was travelling in Donegal. Now, no one who has not been there can form any conception of the wild desolation of this district. There is a little oasis of civilisation round the inn at Gweedore, which was built by Lord George Hill a good many years ago, and is well known to salmon-fishers ; but otherwise you may traverse the whole county and find yourself as completely out of the world as if you were in the back-woods of Canada. You may drive on an outside car—the only means of locomotion —for twenty or thirty Irish miles, over abso-lutely desolate moorland and bog, without seeing a trace of man or woman, bird or beast. Now and then you may perceive, rising out of nothing, as it were, and mov-ing about what is called a 'farm,' but is really only a mud hut, creatures that remind you of the aborigines of Australia or Africa —their big eyes gleaming from under a shock of unkempt hair, and their few poor rags barely held together—a mere apology for clothing.

It was not always so. Once upon a time —I know not how long ago—a peasant could obtain, for a penny, or three-halfpence an acre, a few acres of bogland, which he proceeded to reclaim, digging out sods wherewith to build a cabin for himself and his family, and by draining, burning, and what not, converting its surroundings into usable arable land. Then, too, they had extensive rights of grazing on the mountains, and the wool of the Donegal sheep is the finest and softest known, while the Donegal women are the best knitters in all Ireland. Travellers even from distant Lancashire used to attend the fairs and buy the cottage industries of the farmers' wives and daughters.

But now all this is changed, and the kind stranger lady was touched to the heart by the destitution she saw—borne, too, with such dignity and uncomplaining patience. 'We drove 400 miles through the country,' Mr. Hart writes, 'and though the people were actually starving, we were never begged from but once. Work, work, was all they clamoured for.' Their sturdy morality was refreshing. Here, as everywhere in Ireland, existed the strong purity which characterises the Irish peasant. In the village of Gweedore, during sixty years, one instance only was known of a girl losing her character. There, too, nearly the whole of the adult population were pledged teetotallers, and their honesty was proverbial. 'Surely,' Mrs. Hart adds, 'such a people are worth saving.'

And, with her husband's help—he furnishing the money and she the practical business labour—she tried to save them. She revived the industries once pursued in the district—

spinning, weaving, knitting, sewing, and embroidery. She organised centres where the women were supplied with materials and taught how best to use them, and where their work was brought to be punctually examined, criticised, and paid for. The men, too, were encouraged to recommence hand-loom weaving, and shown how to obtain permanent and beautiful dyes from the bog-plants hard by, so as to produce friezes, tweeds, and serges entirely of home manufacture. 'The great recommendation of them,' says Mrs. Hart, 'is their genuineness. Nothing but wool can be used, for the peasants have nothing else to use. No cheapening admixture of jute and cotton is possible : they are hand-carded, hand-spun, hand-woven, hand-washed and shrunken ; in fact, hand-made from beginning to end.'

Gradually the useful developed into the beautiful. There were a number of Irish

ladies of culture and condition starving like
the peasants. For these Mrs. Hart insti-
tuted the Kells Art embroideries—in which
dyed and polished threads of flax are worked
into Irish linen—after patterns chiefly taken
from the well-known book of Kells. These,
made into table-cloths and table-napkins,
dresses, children's pinafores, curtains, and
portières, are, since they wash perfectly,
available for all domestic use as well as
artistic satisfaction of the eye.

But Mrs. Hart had her difficulties. She
soon saw that, even had it been possible to
build manufactories, this unsystematic, scattered, agrarian population could never have
been brought to work at them. Indeed, it
was not easy to make them work at anything
regularly and with accuracy. The women,
beautifully as they knitted, could not be
taught to see that a pair of socks must be
of exactly the same length, and that colours

must match, and orders be obeyed literally. That fatal ' Oh, it'll do !'—common to other folk than Irish — had to be remorselessly counteracted, and the workers compelled to see that no work 'will do' unless it is as perfect as it can be made.

Mrs. Hart was remorseless : every true teacher must be. Her aim was not that of giving charity, but of helping people to help themselves, so as to have no need of charity. By unlimited patience she contrived to make the work so good, and at the same time so reasonable, that the buyer was as much benefited as the worker. Among large London houses and elsewhere she succeeded in getting a regular sale for her productions, and in distributing in Donegal, as payment, a sum of money which, during a severe winter, saved a whole district from starving. Of course she gained nothing herself. Her working capital brought in no interest, but she kept a list of all her *employés*, ready to give them a bonus, over and above their payment, should circumstances allow.

Hitherto her scheme had been carried on with the aid of a committee ; but she began to see—in committees one often does—that 'everybody's business is nobody's business,' so she took it all into her own hands. She set up a shop — first near Portland Place, then at 43 Wigmore Street—where the sale of Irish work was carried on upon true business principles. There it still is: and an admirable and beautiful shop too. No impossible cheapness allures the stingy purchaser ; nor is any one asked to buy rubbish ' out of charity.' True charity is to provide work for those that need it—work for which the buyer gets the fair value of his money ; neither less nor more. Any other system than this is sure to fail.

But Mrs. Hart's scheme has not failed. Donegal House is, in business phrase, a 'flourishing concern.' The money which goes from it to Donegal county goes not as alms, but honest pay for honest work.

And here I cannot help quoting from Mrs. Hart's 'Letter to her Workers,' whose number is now more than hundreds—thousands. It is dated 'July 1885,' and is remarkable for its terse simplicity, its practical common-sense, and womanly feeling. After recapitulating all she has done—and adding, 'Since I came to Donegal in May 1883, I have never ceased for a single day to think and care for you '—she goes on to a businesslike statement of affairs :

'During the past years I have spent £650 in yarns sent to Donegal, and have paid my knitters £365 for knitting 12,300 pairs of socks and stockings. I have also bought of you 4954 yards of tweed and flannel, paying each spinner and weaver separately for their work. In the past twelve months I have paid over £1000 to my knitters, spinners, weavers, and embroiderers. In parts where wool has been scarce I have sent fleeces, and in every possible way I have striven to keep your looms and spinning-wheels at work. Altogether, I have laid out nearly £2000 in the effort to help you; which sum of money now lies locked up in the various articles you have made and been paid for, but which, as yet, have not been all sold.'

She then goes on to explain that it is easier to make things in Donegal than to sell them in London, and asks her workers to 'have patience' if she cannot give them as many orders as she could wish; though of ultimate success in making these cottage industries self-supporting she has not a doubt.

'But,' she adds, 'that these good times should come depends much upon yourselves, and upon the quality and finish of your work. Everything must be done by you as well as it can possibly be done. It is no use casting on sixty stitches when sixty-five are ordered, or making a sock ten inches long when ten and a half are ordered. By such mistakes the work is made unsaleable and returned on my hands, thereby causing me heavy loss, and you also, for the business is carried on for your interest and your profit, not mine. In everything you must show the greatest care and neatness. Nothing will do, my friends, but the *very best.*'

And any one who will take the trouble to go to Donegal House may soon see that the work there is of the very best. In examining the dainty under-linen, trimmed with beautiful embroidery, it is difficult to believe that it was sent, just as it is, from such wild regions as Glen Esk and Glen Veagh, and made in cabins little better than an English cow-shed.

At any rate, Donegal House proves that the Irish peasant can work and will work, if taken rightly in hand, with a hand at once tender and firm—as we treat our children. For what is the untutored, half-civilised human being of any age but a child? And the Irish nature, above all, is strangely child-like, both in its virtues and its faults.

Mrs. Hart says, in answer to the question, 'Are your people grateful?' 'Nothing is more certain to lead to disappointment than to expect gratitude.' And yet she wins it. A heap of letters is now in my hands—from the ill-spelt, almost undecipherable scrawl of the poor knitter or crochet maker, to the letter of the 'lady of title,' thankful to do Kells embroidery, and the 'mistress,' living almost in starvation upon her own estate, imploring any kind of work 'to get a crust for her old age,' and explaining that she can 'stand a great deal without requiring rest'

—but all these are too pathetic and too sacred to be made public.

That the Irish nature, even in its most untutored type, is amenable to reason, sensitive to kindness, and capable of high moral virtues which, by evil influence, have often been turned into vices, this experiment of Mrs. Hart's has plainly proved. Also, that it is possible to expend capital in Ireland without hopelessly losing it. No doubt the Celtic race is a difficult one to deal with. You must take it by its heart rather than its head ; trust its emotions rather than its self-interest and worldly prudence. You must lead it and guide it without letting it see that it is either led or driven. Nevertheless, while you may smile at or blame it, in many things you cannot fail to respect it. What English or Scotch village could be named in which, as at Gweedore, during sixty years there has been but one fallen woman ? What country town is there where, as in the Donegal famine times, a heap of furniture, brought in exchange for meal, lay whole months in the market-place, no one laying on it a dishonest finger? These facts, which criticisers and calumniators never hear, all suggest the one question raised by Mrs. Hart : Is not Ireland worth saving ?

And though she wisely never looks for gratitude, she finds it. 'When I was in Donegal last year,' she says, ' I went to see Mrs. —— (an agent and knitter). I pulled up at a forlorn village, went in and asked a fat, slatternly, barefooted woman if she were Mrs. ——. " Yes," she replied rather sulkily. " Well, I am Mrs. Hart." Her expression suddenly changed ; she grasped me with both hands : " You, Mrs. Hart ? I would kiss ye if I were *claner !*" Then turning to the women standing about (alas ! poor idle Irishwomen *will* " stand about " by the hour together), she bade them "come and look at the lady who sent ye that blessed work."'

Work, work! Wherever she went that was always the cry. They clamoured for it; they implored for it; and when they got it they did it. In wild, half-civilised Donegal is not at all the feeling which I have heard attributed to great masses of the London unemployed—that they will rather beg three-pence than earn a shilling. The starving Irish peasant, and especially his wife, desires to work. In addition to the thousands on Mrs. Hart's list, the daily applications to her are ceaseless, and sometimes almost heartbreaking, for they must be denied. It would be no true charity to make sup-ply exceed demand; and mere charity—in-discriminate almsgiving—always ends in pauperisation.

At this especial crisis, when Ireland is the topic in everybody's mouth—standing, like a naughty child at the whipping-post, in all her rags and dirt, her sulkiness, anger, and ignorance, while Society seems divided as to whether she ought to be beaten, bound, perhaps even stoned to death, or kissed and coaxed with hypocritical lenity into better behaviour—at this time, I say, it behoves those who think the truth lies between these two lines of conduct to say so, and to back their belief by facts.

Such I have here given, and any one who goes to Donegal House may prove it. For this is not a party question, or a political and religious question. Mrs. Hart's customers and workers are of every possible shade of opinion. She wants no charity, and asks none. All she wants is to save Ireland, as many a human being has been saved, by giving her the great blessing of life—work!

OUR ISLAND SPORTS

—and most insularly primitive they were—
would have been regarded with mild disdain
at Lord's, or Lilliebridge, or any other,
athletic centre in 'the adjacent islands of
Great Britain and Ireland.' But in our
Scottish island—our dear Atlantis of the
West—we thought them very grand indeed.
All our rank, wealth, beauty, and fashion,
migratory and resident, turned out to look at
them, while our aboriginal working population had for weeks beforehand been exercised
in preparing for that one· day of play. A
heavenly day it was, such as makes this our
Golden Island as beautiful as any southern
paradise.

Deep-meadowed, happy, fair with orchard-lawns,
And bowery hollows crowned with summer seas.

Some of the party had watched its dawn from a peak three thousand feet high, having started at one in the morning in the dim moon-set, rowed across the bay, and climbed the mountain by starlight, just in time for a gorgeous sunrise, descending thence triumphantly to breakfast, and professing themselves ' ready for anything.'

Which we elders scarcely were, for you can't go to bed at two and rise at seven, with a party of young Alpine climbers on your mind, without feeling a trifle sleepy afterwards.   But we roused ourselves, and enjoyed fully the drive along the shore, and up the beautiful 'String' road, which winds like a thread over the hillside, visible for miles.   Along its usually solitary line were moving all sorts of equipages—spring-carts, dog-carts, waggonettes—objects of surprise and admiration to one who remembers when almost the only mode of locomotion on the island, except 'gude shanks-naigie,' was a sort of rude cart without any springs at all. To be jolted in it along this String road was a martyrdom compared to which the longest walk became a luxury.

We had thought that to sit still for two hours in a comfortable carriage would be a desirable rest for our mountaineers. Not a bit of it! They never seem to know what rest is, except when asleep in their beds. They kept jumping out at every available instant, to relieve the horses, they said, but also, I believe, to get rid of their own exuberant vitality. And every five minutes they turned to look tenderly at the lofty peak whence they had just descended, and remark with patronising calmness of every beautiful view that was pointed out to them, 'Oh! we've seen it before—at five this morning.

Truly, to watch the sunrise from a mountain-top makes a person intolerably conceited for a week after.

So thought those who fain would go and never can, but must watch mountains from the humble plain for the rest of their days. Only, what a good thing it is to have a mountain to watch, and eyes to see it !

The—village, shall I call it ? as it consists merely of a roadside inn, a farm, and a few scattered cottages, had never till now arrived at the dignity of having sports at all, and felt itself important accordingly. There was quite a bustle in front of the little 'public.' Its yard was filled with vehicles, and before its door were rows of white-covered tables, inquirers being informed that accommodation could only be had 'outside.' Inside, the comfortable-looking landlady and pleasant-faced lassie, who had to do everything between them, seemed overladen with re-

sponsibility, but yet prepared to meet
it all.

So half of us relieved them by walking off
with our provision basket, and eating our
dinner in peace by the side of a burn, leaving
the others, who preferred luxury and hot
meat, to make the best of it; which was
better than they expected, for they met us
half an hour after with cheerful countenances,
declaring they had dined capitally. And
dinner, let me confess, in our dear island,
where food is limited, and appetites are unlimited, is a very important thing. I remember once, coming back from a long walk
which made one ready to 'eat one's hat,' as
they say, being met by an agreeable smile of
true Highland politeness and the regret that
the fish we had ordered 'wadna be caught.'
There was only one egg in the house, though
the hen 'clucked as if she was thinkin' to lay
another.' Could we wait? We did wait,

but the hen changed her mind, and finally we had to dine off porridge and sour milk, consoled by a promise to kill 'half a sheep' for us to-morrow. Whether the other half was to be left running about the mountains till required, did not transpire. We took boat next day to the mainland.

But this happened thirty years ago. Since then, our island has advanced in civilisation most miraculously — sometimes most painfully. Astonishing were the toilettes we followed down the farmyard lane which led to the field, where in a large level plateau the sports were going on. Fashionable polonaises and jackets, hats all feathers and lace, wiggle-waggle dress-improvers, and barbarous high-heeled shoes we saw in plenty; but where was the bright-tinted petticoat and short gown? — the white mutch with the plaid drawn over it?—the tartan and the kilt? Gone, all gone! Not a single trace

of the old Highland costume could we discover, and we mourned over our Islanders
fallen from their high estate of picturesque
simplicity, and melting into the light of
common day.

Still, the natural beauty of the scene could
not be spoiled.   Our artist, leaning against a
gate, took it all in, despairing to set it down
—the horse-shoe circle of spectators keenly
interested, the accidental groups moving outside, and the sunshiny sleepy repose of the
mountains beyond, each standing in his place
through gloom or shine.   No 'Lord's' or
'Lilliebridge' could rival them.

The honest ground was the only seat provided for everybody, except a rude platform
covered with a bit of brilliant, but not too
artistic, carpet, where were placed, *pro tem.*,
the musicians—a harp, cornet, and violin—
who gave us 'Who'll be king but Charlie?'
'A wee bird came to our ha' door,' 'The

Auld House,' and other known tunes, with a pathos and energy, as well as skill, often wanting in much grander bands; and when they subsided into modern music they did equally well, though it was rather funny to hear the *Iolanthe* and *Patience* airs in our far-away island.

But, except ourselves, no one seemed to listen much; all were absorbed in the high jump then going on. Youth after youth, lithe and wiry, though scarcely so graceful as our southern athletes, cleared the pole, almost as high as themselves. At each success there was a hearty shout; at each of the few failures a good-natured laugh. Evidently the competitors were all showing off under the eyes of their 'ain folk,' which much increased the excitement.

It reached its pitch when a long line of young men were tied by the leg in twos and twos, to run the comical three-legged race,

which always delights children and the child-
like populace. None sported the brilliant, if
rather limited running costume familiar to
English athletes, but wore just their ordinary
coloured shirt, and trousers tucked up to the
knee; yet there were some fine Greek forms
among them, which our artist hastily sketched.
And when, at the sound of a pistol shot, they
all started, wild were the shouts, in Gaelic and
English, that followed them; and loud was
the cry, half howl, half cheer, which rang
across the field, when they all fell together, a
writhing mass of legs and arms, in front of
a winning-post. One couple lay there some
minutes, and when unbound were seen to be
examined so anxiously that a whisper of
'Leg broken' ran round the admiring circle,
and an ardent disciple of St. John's Ambu-
lance Society was just about to advance,
proffering 'first aid to the wounded,' when
the young man rose up and walked away..

Putting the stone and throwing the caber are performances exclusively Scottish. Only Highland thews and sinews, frames hardened by mountain air and porridge, and innocent of beef and beer—Hodge, poor fellow, is too apt to overeat as well as overdrink himself if he gets a chance—only such brawny fellows as these could have 'putted' so accurately and so far a twenty-pound lump of solid granite, or poised with such amazing. steadiness and then thrown over in a double somersault a huge pine-tree that might have served as walking-stick to the 'monster Polypheme.' One man (I believe a gamekeeper—and if so, woe to the poacher who had to wrestle with him!) 'putted' the stone again and again; another, gray-haired, but Herculean still, balanced the caber, and ran along with it for a few yards before throwing it over, in a way perfectly marvellous to our Saxon eyes.

By this time, the excited throng of natives
had been increased by a good number better
dressed and calmer minded — tourists and
holiday folk. It was amusing to notice what
really charming costumes had been fished out
of portmanteaus and chests of drawers in
those tiny white 'letting' cottages, which dot
every corner of the island, and where whole
families who have discovered, and, alas! are
discovering more and more every year, what
a delightful island it is, contrive to stow
themselves away for the summer. No gorgeous silks or satins appeared : the dresses
were chiefly of coloured cotton, or pure white
brightened with a 'Liberty' sash ; while many
a pretty face smiled from under a three-half-
penny Zulu hat, decked with a bit of bright
colour, or a bunch of real heather. The
young men too—does a young man ever
look so well as in his gray shooting clothes,
his bonnet and his knickerbockers ? devot-

ing himself to a simply-dressed girl—not a
'young lady'—who brings an almost child-
like element of frank enjoyment into the
natural charm which draws men and young
women together, and will do to the end of
time? And if it ends in something deeper
—well! which is likely to be the best and
safest love, that born in a ballroom or on a
Highland moor?

The children too were especially happy.
I noticed half a dozen groups of slender
damsels with short frocks and long tails,
who may grow up to be the belles of the
next generation. And there was a boy about
twelve, who went about the field dressed in
the roughest of clothes, with his beautiful bare
brown legs and feet shaped like an Antinous,
and a face that might have been that of a
young duke.

And when the aristocratic element really
came upon the scene, it still further exempli-

fied the fact, that the higher you go up in
the social scale the simpler are your manners,
and the less you 'bother' about your clothes.
By and by, the band having vacated the tiny
platform, it was occupied by three ladies,
very quietly attired, and two gentlemen in
shooting costumes. The former had a rough
garden seat provided, the latter sat dangling
their legs over the wooden framework, but
all five seemed thoroughly to enjoy the scene ;
especially the hundred yards race which now
came off, accompanied by shouts of 'Noo,
Thomas!' 'Noo, Donald!' 'Well done,
John!' Everybody seemed to know everybody and to call them by their Christian names.
And no Pythian or Olympian games could have
been watched with greater excitement, while
Hymettus itself could not have furnished a
lovelier background or more picturesque setting to the scene than those soft gray mountains, melting away into the bright blue sky.

'Our artist' was delighted, and eagerly set down every scratch she could, while 'our author,' afraid of forgetting something, begged from two or three friends the smallest scrap of paper to make notes on, and at last received out of a little girl's pocket an old envelope, which was literally 'worth its weight in gold.'

'Look! there's a lady sketching us,' said one of the platform party, happily ignorant of the other enemy silently standing behind.

'Never mind. Let her do it! Which lady?'

'One in pink—very much pink! I must hide, or she'll be sure to take my likeness,' said one young fellow, pretending a fit of shyness. 'I can't stand it. I must run away.'

'Nonsense, stay where you are,' commanded a pleasant-voiced little lady. 'We'll all sit still, and let the artist do what she likes.'

Which she did, and there they are, spectators of the final race, at least so far as they could be done.

The commanding little lady began chatting to the people round the platform. 'And how do you do, Mr. —— ? and is your wife quite well ?' stooping over to shake hands with a very homely person, who blurted out an awkward 'Yes, ma'am,' and was reproved by another man adding pointedly, 'Thank you, your Grace, his wife and daughter are just behind.'

Who were at once brought up and shaken hands with by 'her Grace,' who seemed to know everybody, as of course everybody knew her. Simple in dress and frank in manner, the Duchess among her own island people, to whom she was evidently *the* Duchess, the only Duchess in the world, was a pleasant sight to see, and her own evident enjoyment added to that of those about her.

M

The final show was a horse-race, not at all of the Derby and Ascot type. The competitors were chiefly farm-horses, ridden bare-backed, and the gyrations they made, and the difficulty there was in getting them to start at all, or to keep the assigned course when they had started, proved a source of intense amusement. But there was certainly no betting, no making of 'books,' for the races; it was all honest downright fun. The Duchess, a notable horsewoman, who may be seen all over the moors following the Duke on a shooting pony, was not among the least amused of the spectators.

'Her Grace' is not one of the fashionable beauties, and I never heard whether she is clever or not; but with the afternoon sun shining on her cheerful face under the neat hat, with her simple, pretty muslin gown, and her kind words and smiles for every-body about her, our Duchess was really a credit to her strawberry leaves. Her islanders, in their sturdy, independent, yet truly Highland devotion, evidently thought so. They neither intruded upon her, nor stared at her, but every one when addressed by her unhesitatingly put forth his right hand, which she as frankly accepted.

And now the afternoon sun began to slant westward, and various groups were seen to sit down and attack bags of biscuits or 'cookies,' or retiring across the fields in search of tea, the only beverage available, for the Duke wisely discourages the sale of alcoholic drinks throughout the island. Consequently it is, for a whisky-loving race, a tolerably sober island.[1] You may go about

[1] Two days after writing this, alas! the lives of our whole party—twelve in all—were risked by two drunken car-drivers. But it was, as in many other cases, partly the fault of the 'strangers.' Certain visitors, while the men were drinking, had tempted them beyond their power of resistance. I cannot too strongly condemn the universal Highland practice of giving 'drams.' The Celtic nature is

it at any hour of the day or night and never meet a drunken man or woman. Nor, though it is scarcely a wealthy community, do you ever witness in it that squalid poverty, that total degradation of manners and morals, which, alas! is not wholly confined to towns. We also, spurred on by hunger, began to think we would omit the end of the sports, and be beforehand with the world in getting tea at the all-important inn. Already symptoms of frolic being over and work begun appeared in the shape of a lovely herd of cows brought in to be milked, which the farmer, the same burly old fellow with whom the Duchess had shaken hands, hastened to see after, turning back more than once to

a strange mixture of laziness and energy, exceeding love of pleasure, yet an almost miraculous endurance of hardship and pain. Every tourist who indulges in whisky himself, or gives it to his inferiors,—who treats drunkenness as a joke instead of an absolute crime, and the cause of no end of crime,—every such man is most seriously to blame, much more so than our luckless car-drivers.

shout in an anxious voice, to a slim and stylish and ultra-fashionable young lady, 'Annie! Annie! dinna forget to take up the bull.'

Highland bulls are proverbially mild of nature, yet we quickened our pace up the lane to the inn-door, where, by great favour, the landlady condescended to give us tea downstairs, the parlour upstairs being made ready for the Duchess. A very dainty tea-table it looked, when we dared to peer in— bread and butter, scones and cakes, jam and honey—as we knew to our cost, when, asking for honey, we were told that there was only one tiny pot to be had, 'and the Duchess had got it.'

We did not grudge it to her. We only hoped she would enjoy her tea, for she de-served it. She had spent a whole afternoon in sharing her people's pleasure, making others happy and herself too, let us hope— for these things are always mutual.

One of the strongest impressions left by these Island Sports of ours was the relationship between the lord of the soil and his people, a sort of feudal friendship, existing for generations, and riveted by the present generation into a tie of respectful devotion, often most touching to see. Every face brightens when you speak of the Duke and Duchess, whose yearly arrival at their ancestral castle and at the two smaller houses which they have on the other side of the island is hailed with enthusiasm. 'The Duke knows personally every tenant he has,' was said one day. And as for the Duchess, when, after years of waiting, her Grace came that year with a little Lady Mary, a nine-months-old baby, there was not a mother on the island who did not seem as proud as if the child had been her own.

It is the personal relation, the power to see the master's face and shake the mistress's hand, to interchange all the small charities which are so great a bond between rich and poor, avoiding patronising on the one hand, and subserviency on the other—it is these things which make the tie between land-owners and land-labourers so pleasant and so secure. But the duty—a duty as momentous in its degree as that from child to parent, parent to child,—must be accepted as such, not only believed in but fulfilled.

Would that this lesson could be taught in another island, within a few hours' sail of this happy island of ours! one which ought to be, so great are its possibilities, 'first flower of the earth and first gem of the sea,' yet which is—we all know what! Is there no noble or gentle blood in Ireland, people of 'the ould stock,' for which the genuine Irishman, like the Highlander, has an almost blind attachment, which would warm to the sod? feeling that to live even a portion of every year among one's own people does more to calm the popular mind and win the national heart than hosts of legal enactments; that a resident landlord is better than a whole staff of constabulary, and a kindly-faced woman like our Duchess, going about shaking hands with rough men, would likely have more power over them than any rabid demagogue?

Demagogues could not exist in our Golden Island. It has but one enemy—that accursed foe which a man puts into his mouth to take away his brains. But to-day at least it was absent. After our harmless tea in the inn parlour, watching various other families enjoying the same innocent meal on the benches outside, we drove home through the still twilight, congratulating ourselves and the island on one fact, that throughout all the sports we had seen no sign of a single drop of whisky.

MERELY PLAYERS

> All the world's a stage,
> And all the men and women merely players,

which accounts for the fact that we all of us
—or almost all, especially those of simple,
childlike, and imaginative natures—delight
in a play, and are apt to get up an ardent
enthusiasm for those 'poor players,'

> Who strut and fret their hour upon the stage,
> And then are seen no more.

Nor is this wonderful. To be able to throw
one's self completely out of one's self into
another's individuality is one of the highest
triumphs of intellectual art. The painter
does it, in degree, when he invents a face
and depicts it, real as life, though it exists

only in his own fancy; the novelist does it, by thinking out a character, and making his puppet act and speak according to its nature and its surrounding circumstances. But the actor is both these combined. He must look the picture, he must be the character. Therefore a truly great actor in any line— whether he stirs in us the heroic pain of tragedy, or refreshes us with harmless comedy, or even by the fun of broad farce 'shoots Folly as it flies'—is, in his generation, among the best benefactors of society.

All the more so, perhaps, because his life-work is of so ephemeral a kind. The artist leaves his pictures, the author his books, behind him, for the world to judge him by, and to profit from, long after he is gone; the actor leaves behind him only a memory. No description can keep alive, even for a single generation, the fame of that fascination which once drove audiences wild with

delight. It is gone — vanished!—as completely as an ended song, a forgotten dream.
Who now believes in Mrs. Siddons's grace,
John Kemble's dignity, Edmund Kean's
pathos and passion? Nay, the young generation begins to smile when we, who have
seen him, praise Macready. They think he
was, after all, nothing to compare to Henry
Irving. And how can we prove anything?
We can only say, ' It was so.'

It is this which makes the underlying
pathos of acting, and the actor's life—the feeling of ' Live while you live, for to-morrow
all will have passed away.' Still, while it
lasts, the charm is all-powerful, the triumph
supreme. No admired author or artist, no
victorious general or popular sovereign, ever
evokes such universal enthusiasm, or receives
such passionate ovations, as a successful
actor and actress during their brief day—
brief, but still glorious and great in its power

for good or for evil.   Those of us who can
recall the enthusiasms of our youth,—how we
used to come home from the play, literally
saturated—soaked through and through—
with insane admiration ; hearing for days the
tones of the one voice, imitating and quoting
the words and gestures of our idol,—must
confess that it is a high and a responsible
career even to be 'merely players.'

I am led to these remarks by reading
through—and it takes a good deal, perhaps
a little too much, of reading — a volume
entitled, *Some of Shakespeare's Female
Characters*, by Helen Faucit, Lady Martin.
Truly, if any one has a right to say her say
on these said characters, and to be listened
to, it is Lady Martin.

For forty years, possibly more, since she rose
early and set late, Helen Faucit was the star
of our English, and especially of our Shakespearian drama.   Among the last generation

of actresses there was no one to compare
with her.   More refined and cultivated than
Miss Glyn, though in genius and passion few
could surpass the occasional outbursts of that
very remarkable woman ; more original and
free from mannerisms than Mrs. Charles Kean
and Miss Vandenhoff; while those passing
meteors, Fanny Kemble and Mrs. Scott
Siddons, can scarcely be counted as rivals—
Helen Faucit remains, to all of us who have
lived long enough to contrast the present
with the past, the best impersonator of
Shakespeare's women whom the last generation has ever seen.

Though not beautiful, there was about her
an atmosphere of beauty, which made itself
felt as soon as ever she came on the stage.
Her lightest gesture, the first tone of her
voice, heard through all other stage voices
like a thrush through a chorus of sparrows,
seemed part of a harmonious whole.   She

had no sharp angles, no accidental outbursts, which may be either pathos or bathos, just as it happens ; everything with her was artistically perfect.   If, as some alleged, too perfect —that in her care never to 'outstep the modesty of nature' she ignored nature altogether, and substituted art—it was at any rate a very high form of art.   And after reading her book, which gives us a glimpse into the soul of the woman, for it is essentially a woman's book, we come to the conclusion that the secret of her success was not art but nature.   She felt all she acted.   Her cultivated mind, which, if not absolutely poetic, had a sympathetic appreciation of poetry, enabled her to take in all the delicate *nuances* of Shakespeare's characters, while her heart taught her to understand those things which have made 'Shakespeare's women' a proverb for feminine charm. During a whole generation—nay, more, for, like Ninon de l'Enclos, she seemed to have perpetual youth—she so enchained the public that the children and grandchildren of her first worshippers were her worshippers too. And she retired with none but physical graces lost. Her Portia and Rosalind, acted when she must have been over sixty, were delightful still. Such an actress cannot but have had as the key to her popularity, the only key which unlocks 'the wide heart of humanity,' a heart of her own.

This book shows it, and makes interesting what as a literary production might have been superfluous, for Shakespeare has had only too many commentators and analysers. But here we have an individual study, not of the whole play, but of the one character in it which the actress impersonated. In a very simple and feminine way, autobiographical without being egotistic, she lets us into the secrets of that impersonation. We see how she must have penetrated—for herself and not another, since she tells us she had never seen them acted by any other—into the very nature of Juliet, Desdemona, Imogen, and caught the bright spirit of Rosalind and Beatrice—though she owns she never cared for these last as she did for the more womanly women. If, in truth, she takes too feminine a view of her poet,—if in the minuteness of her criticism she attributes to Shakespeare's women certain nineteenth century qualities which Shakespeare never thought of, and embellishes them with preceding and subsequent episodes wholly imaginary, such as Ophelia's motherless childhood, and Portia's consolatory visit to the dying Shylock,—we forgive her, since she has made a contribution to Shakespearian literature quite original of its kind, and which could have been done thus by no other person.

With the exception of an appendix of

French and English criticisms, which might well have been omitted, it is a book, for an actress, strangely impersonal. We wish indeed it had been a little more of an auto-biography. So many players are 'merely players,' with no literary capacity at all, no means of expressing their feeling about their art or their method of study, that such revelations from a woman of Lady Martin's intellectual calibre would have been not only pleasant but profitable. Now that we see her no more, it is interesting to an almost pathetic degree to hear that in her first girlish performance of Juliet, her nervousness was such that she crushed the phial in her hand, and never discovered this till she saw the blood - drops staining her white dress; how Macready complained that she was 'so hard to kill' as Desdemona; and how, when writing about Imogen, the remembered agony seemed still to

N

fill her mind, as it used to do on the stage.

As a whole this book, and the light it throws both upon the individuality and the professional history of the writer, are to us, who remember what Helen Faucit was, and the sort of plays she acted in, a curious contrast to the stage and the actors of to-day. Then Browning, Westland Marston, Milman, G. W. Lovell, Bulwer Lytton, were, if not all poets, at least very capable dramatists, who had no need to steal from the French, but could invent actable plays, which intelligent audiences eagerly listened to, and went home the better for it. The writing might have been a little stilted, lengthy, and didactic, and the acting more conventional than realistic, but the tone was always pure and high. No confusion of right and wrong made you doubt whether it was criminal or only 'funny' to make love to

your neighbour's wife ; or whether, instead
of the old-fashioned stage morality, when
virtue was rewarded and vice punished,
there was not now a system of things much
more interesting, in which a lady of no
virtue to speak of, and a gentleman who
prided himself on breaking all the ten com-
mandments, were the hero and heroine with
whom you were expected to sympathise. Is
it so now ? To how many—or rather how
few—London theatres can one take one's
young daughters and sons without blushing
for them—and ourselves ?

All the worse because over the foulness
is thrown a certain veneer of refinement.
Shakespeare, though often coarse in language,
as was the fashion of his time, is always
pure at heart—pure as the Bible itself, which
is perhaps the plainest-spoken book of that
date now admitted into general reading.
His women, too, spite of our ultra-realistic

modern actresses — one of whom as Juliet appears on the stage *en robe de nuit*, and another sings an interpolated song which Shakespeare never would have put in the mouth of his maidenly and pure - minded Rosalind — his women are and always will be the ideal of all feminine purity. Except the historical Cleopatra, there is not among all his diverse heroines one unchaste woman. Imagine the creator of Imogen, Desdemona, Portia, inventing a Dame aux Camélias, a Fédora, or a Théodora!

Such a book as this of Lady Martin's awakes in us, with a regretful memory of what the stage was, a longing for what it ought to be and might be. Not exactly by returning to old traditions; the world is for ever advancing, and we must accommodate ourselves to this fact. Even lately a charming little comedy of Westland Marston's, *Under Fire*, which for wit and grace of diction, and delicate sketches of character, was worth a dozen ephemeral and immoral French vaudevilles, fell flat after two or three nights. And not even its admirable *mise-en-scène* and the perfect acting of Wilson Barrett could save the public from discovering that Bulwer's *Junius* was an essentially false diamond, which the most splendid setting could never rescue from deserved oblivion. No! 'The old order changeth, giving place to new,' and it is right it should be so. Only, let us try that the new 'order' be as good as the old.

Dramatic art at present may be roughly divided into three sections: the Shakespearian and poetic drama, melodrama, and adaptations from the French. A few stray variations, English and original, may crop up between, such as the evergreen *Our Boys;* but still, putting aside the drama proper, and melodrama in its modern phase of domestic realism, the stock *repertoire* of managers and actors both in London and the provinces is almost exclusively 'stolen' from our neighbours across the Channel. Whether the theft is to our benefit or their credit remains an open question.

Of high art dramas, not Shakespearian, there are, alas! not many; yet audiences 'fit though few' have had the sense to appreciate *The Cup* and *The Falcon*. Poets are not often, nor necessarily, skilled playwrights, for a play is poetry in action, rather than diction. But if they would condescend to this limitation and train themselves into writing for the stage, which is quite different from writing for the closet, there seems no reason why our nineteenth century should not give us a second Shakespeare, if audiences could be educated into intelligent appreciation of him. I lately overheard an actor conversing with an author on the lack of English talent, and

the flood of French triviality, in the modern
drama. The actor—he was one of those
cultivated, high-minded gentlemen, men with
an ideal, who are gradually ennobling the
profession—said to the author, ' People lay
all this to the charge of the managers and
actors, but it is not so. We want audiences.
Not the "gilded youth," or the man about
town who merely goes to the theatre to
amuse himself, but an audience, intelligent,
appreciative, critical without being ill-natured,
composed of fathers and mothers of families,
who come with their sons and daughters, and
spend their money as regularly and safely
upon the theatre as upon Mudie's Library.
To them the stage should be not a mere
amusement, but a part of education, supported
and deserving of support by cultivated,
intelligent, and right-minded people, instead
of by the froth, or worse than the froth—the
vicious residuum of society.'

Most true, and yet I think this actor, who was still young and enthusiastic in his profession, laid the saddle on the wrong horse. May not the fault lie primarily with managers and actors? The public is like a child, as simple and as impressionable. You must either be led by it or lead it, and it rather prefers the latter, if any one is strong enough to do this—to take the bull Society by the horns, and beginning as a revolutionist, to end as an autocrat.

Could there not be established in London —I believe there is in New York—a theatre of which the primary object is that nothing shall be allowed therein which sins against morality or decorum? thereby abolishing at once the unwholesome atmosphere which makes the modern stage often a place which no decent woman or honest man can breathe in? Failing this, could not our best actors and actresses, many of them excellent fathers and devoted wives and mothers, take the law into their own hands—absolutely refuse to act in such plays as we outsiders shrink from taking our young daughters to see? And if, besides pure morality, high art was also studied—and by high art I mean the best of everything, be it a *lever de rideau* or a broad farce, all being done as well as it could be done, not merely to please, but to elevate the public—would such a theatre fail? Pessimists say it would: but I for one think better of human nature. I believe it would in a very short time be crammed nightly to the ceiling.

There is a vast and virtuous understratum in society which really loves the right and hates the wrong. In proof of this we need only point to modern Shakespeare revivals, always successful in any theatre, and to that form of melodrama which, on the principle that everything excellent of its kind *is* high art, ranks only second to what is called the legitimate drama.

No one could go and see such pieces as *Chatterton*, *The Silver King*, and even the *Lights o' London*, without coming away the better—morally as well as mentally. So far as it goes, each is thoroughly well acted throughout—a veritable transcript of nature. Though realism is sometimes carried to excess. A van with live horses crossing the stage, the outside of a gin palace, the inside of a London 'slum,' though vivid and life-like as some Dutch painting of a drunken boor, may all be questionable subjects for art at all. But on the whole these melodramas are admirable studies of nature, and nature always wins. For among the generality of middle-class playgoers there is an honest sense of right and wrong, a delight in seeing virtue rewarded and vice punished, very refreshing to see.

But the artist in any branch cannot rely
on nature only. He must use that power of
selection which is the secret of genius, and
use nature without abusing it. Surely between the intensely realistic and the poetical
drama there must lie a golden mean, which
if managers and actors would believe in, their
fortunes would be made. Witness the enormous success of that very original play,
Claudian. Its pure idealism, lofty moral,
nay, actual religiousness of tone, caught the
popular fancy, and it 'ran' for a year and a
half.

Let sceptics howl as they will, there is
still in our England a wholesome heart of
righteousness—the recoil of pure-minded
women and chivalric men against that foul
sewage stream which sometimes threatens to
swamp us all. Every one who helps to stem
it does a good deed. Therefore, those who,
though 'play-actors,' are also gentlemen and

gentlewomen, striving both by their acting and their private lives to make the stage what it ought to be, may take consolation for the brevity of their day of fame by remembering that while it lasts their power to guide not only public taste but public morality is enormous. And it is a personal power. Individual character as well as genius is the root of it. No woman who was not good, pure, and high - minded could have impersonated Shakespeare's women as Helen Faucit used to do. And though I have carefully avoided referring to those others of her profession who are still before the public, it would be easy to name a noble band of rising and risen actors and actresses, whom the British public—that is, the worthiest section of it—would certainly not admire as it does if it could not say between its bursts of enthusiasm, 'That man is a true gentle-

man,' 'That woman is a thoroughly good
woman.'

If this is not always so, God help them,
and God pity them!—for the small mimic
stage has double temptations compared with
the larger stage of the world. Shakespeare
knew both—he was an actor as well as an
author, and yet he could paint a Desdemona,
an Imogen, a Hamlet, a Coriolanus. When
our modern dramatists aim at creating such
characters, and our modern actors and
actresses delight in impersonating them,
believing that to show Vice her own image
is infinitely more dangerous than to hide it,
or shame her by showing the ideal image of
Virtue, then will the impressionable public
believe that there really is a charm worth
trying for in 'whatsoever things are pure,
whatsoever things are holy,' or even only
'of good report.' Thus, and thus only, we
may hope for the gradual purifying of the

stage, and the raising into the goodly company of true artists those whom some of us
are prone to condemn or ignore as 'merely
players.'

MISS ANDERSON IN THE
'WINTER'S TALE'

I HAVE been a playgoer for over forty years, during which I have seen many a star rise and set—in fact, the whole dramatic hemisphere has changed; and there have been countless alterations, some for the better, and some for the worse. But my hearty love and appreciation of histrionic art has never altered; I now feel a play as keenly as a girl of sixteen—while bringing to it also the cool criticism of a lifetime's experience; therefore I think I may be listened to in a matter wherein the London critics seem to have been very unfair.

I did not join in the first *furore* over Miss

Mary Anderson. She appeared to me a beautiful, intelligent, and attractive woman; but whether she would ever make a great actress remained to be proved. It depended upon her being able to keep a steady head, in spite of popular admiration—so as to attain by patient and continuous study that dramatic culture without which beauty and even genius are absolutely useless. Her Parthenia and Galatea, though graceful sketches, scarcely led up to Juliet—a part of which a great actress once said, 'We can never understand it till we are too old to play it.' No wonder, therefore, though she looked it to perfection, and was charming in the lighter scenes, that Miss Anderson failed to attain the tragic height of the sixteen-year-old girl of Verona. Rosalind, played just before she left for America, was the first indication of her capacity to impersonate Shakespeare's heroines. The fantastic lovelorn boy-girl, witty and winning, yet never losing her maiden dignity, was played by her better than by anybody since Helen Faucit. She seemed to have in her that rare combination of nature and art, the poet's instinct and the woman's soul, without which no actress need attempt those women of women—Shakespeare's.

Therefore when she came back and announced her daring, unique, and ingenious combination of Hermione and Perdita— mother and daughter—in the *Winter's Tale*, I was eager to see her; all the more because the newspaper critics were against her. But a press verdict is not infallible. I have seen many a poor play and actor written up, many a good one written down, and both at last always found their right level. Most of the objections and condemnations were futile and unnecessary. For instance, the doubling of the parts, so much complained of as 'con-

o

fusion,' caused, I found, only the omission
of four lines of Perdita's part, and the intro-
duction of a harmless dummy for about three
minutes before the curtain's fall.   The ex-
cisions of words and phrases, which the
natural growth of refinement between the
sixteenth and nineteenth centuries made
necessary, were very few; and, much as
she has been abused, Miss Anderson was
right to make them.   All else she has left
as she found it.   Dear old Will, though he
calls a spade a spade, and deals with human
nature as he saw it—the human nature of his
time—is at heart always pure, always moral.
In him you never find that elegant euphuistic
glossing over of sin, to be laughed at in
comedy and sentimentalised upon in tragedy,
which makes one shrink from taking one's
young daughters to almost any modern play.

The *Winter's Tale* is essentially a tale,
no more.   It goes against all the canons of

dramatic unity, is full of ridiculous anachron-
isms, yet has a human interest and poetic
charm peculiarly its own. Also, it is so
seldom acted that it must have come fresh
to the London critics, startling them, not out
of their proprieties, but out of their impro-
prieties. The picture of a young man and
young woman, bachelor and maid, innocently
and virtuously in love with one another ; of a
wife so consciously pure that she can give the
kiss of welcome to her husband's friend (as
was the custom in Shakespeare's time) without thought of blame, and whose only reproach
to that brutal husband is :

> Adieu, my lord ;
> I never wished to see you sorry—now
> I trust I shall—

was a phase of dramatic interest so new
to the present generation of playgoers and
play-reviewers, that it must have been to
them like a dish of strawberries and cream

after feeding upon 'high'—very high—venison.

No wonder they carped at it, and at the actress who, instead of the Fédoras and Théodoras in tragedy, and the whole range of transplanted French heroines of comedy, had courage to present to the public two such women—merely women—as Hermione and Perdita.

Miss Anderson is not a perfect Hermione, especially in the first scene, when she does not well manage a not always harmonious voice; and her manner is scarcely stately enough for 'the daughter of a king,' the matron-queen whose sweet courtesy to her husband's guest is miles removed from modern 'flirting.' But at once she strikes the keynote of the character—thorough womanliness. Her fondling of Mamillius, her kindliness to her women, her tender playfulness with Leontes, all carry out the true conception of the part. And in the trial scene, when a commoner actress would have given us a ranting tragedy-queen, Miss Anderson is simplicity itself—a wronged, broken-hearted woman, sick and worn, but yet noble in her innocence. Her by-play is excellent, every gesture full of the deepest pathos; and her blank verse—the critics said she did not know how to declaim blank verse—was not 'declaimed' at all, but wrung from her, brokenly and by fits, exactly as in such a case would be.

The only fault in this scene—as fine a one as ever Shakespeare wrote—is her parting look of reproach at her husband, which Miss Anderson would do well to reconsider, or omit entirely.

Another stage 'point' which was severely commented on, and must have seemed strange to an audience accustomed to watch the ravings of heroines, even when *in articulo mortis*, was Hermione's reception of the tidings that her little son is dead. In that supreme agony she neither shrieks nor moans, but stands paralysed a moment (the stony look of her face is a perfect study), then covers her head with her mantle and sinks slowly down. Genius and nature could alone have suggested to Miss Anderson a gesture so pathetic and so real—just like the peasant-woman who throws her apron over her head. Any one who has ever received from fate a blow which seems to turn the living and breathing woman into an image of stone—conscious only of one instinct, how best to conceal it—will acknowledge the truthfulness of the delineation.

It was a bold idea, a critical test, to disappear from an audience thus, and reappear half an hour after as Perdita—

> . . . the prettiest low-born lass that ever
> Danced on the green sward.

That exquisite creature, in whom 'all she does still betters what is done,' was never more exquisitely presented than by Miss Anderson, who, physically, is a perfect Shakespeare's woman. Her beauty, her grace, the almost childlike sweetness of her face and gestures, and an atmosphere of innocent simplicity so completely un-'stagey' take one fairly by storm. We follow her with eager eyes, and truly, when she dances, wish her

> . . . a wave o' the sea,
> That she might do it ever.

If any fault can be found in a study that would have charmed Shakespeare's self, it is that the princess-peasant, being a princess, is a little too like the common herd in her demonstrations of affection for her 'sweet friend' Florizel. A certain reticence and dignity would have marked her most passionate tenderness. By the way, what a pity that Mr. Forbes Robertson, who acts so well the thankless and too elderly part of Leontes, could not also have doubled it with that of Florizel, and so made a true picture of that brave young prince who has the sense to see in the village-girl a royal nature equal to his own, and holds to her with a pure, passionate love and courageous fidelity. Florizel, usually confided to secondary performers, might, in the hands of a really good actor, be an exceedingly useful study of a young man—a pattern to all the young men of to-day, from the 'mashers' in the stalls to the 'Arrys of the gallery.

It is this view of the stage as a great teacher, better than most books and many sermons, which has evoked the present notice of the *Winter's Tale* at the Lyceum. It is a charming spectacle—pleasant to the ear and delightful to the eye; for the artistic *mise-en-scène* is excellent, save the 'dummy' baby ('not a judicious baby,' as one spectator observed), which rouses in the audience an irresistible titter. The music is very good, except for the evil habit our orchestras are getting into of accompanying special bits, thereby spoiling both music and speeches. Besides all this, it is an innocent play. We come from it entirely free from that 'bad taste in one's mouth' with which one generally quits a theatre. Shakespeare, if rough, is always wholesome. In him we never find that condoning and plastering over of vice which is the curse of the modern stage. 'Death is a fearful thing,' says Claudio. 'And shamed life a hateful,' answers Isabella. Nor does he ever make sin anything else than hateful. Dear old Will! even his comedy, when purged of certain verbal grossnesses peculiar to his time, is, as in the *Winter's Tale*, perfectly harmless to pure ears and eyes.

For some months to come, let us hope
there will be at least one theatre in London
where one can take one's young daughters
without tainting their fresh souls by images
of wickedness, or, worse, putting vice in such
pleasant or pathetic shape that they mistake
it for virtue.

Why should it not be so? Why should
not managers (who are, many of them, most
respectable men and women) and actors
(often as good husbands and wives, fathers
and mothers, as any of us all), why should
they not combine to give the omnivorous
British public wholesome food instead of
garbage? Its appetite is wholesome still.
Witness the honest delight with which it
applauds 'virtue rewarded and vice punished.' What crowds went nightly to see
Olivia, Claudian, and the like! And now
every Shakespearian revival may count
upon a lengthened 'run.' Why not give

it good food instead of bad?—provided the food is palatable.

And can it be possible that our honest English brains are unable to produce anything which is palatable without being dull? Are managers so afraid of this that their worst condemnation of a play is (I have known it given), 'Oh! it will never pay; it is *too moral*'?

How, then, can we stem this fatal tide, which is drifting us off into the lowest depths of Greek and Roman degradation? —all the worse because, like them, it has a smooth surface of artistic beauty and refinement. Will no one raise a warning voice (especially to the young generation), 'Take heed where you are going'? And, more, will no one try to arrest them in the fatal way they are going?

We have set aside the old superstition that as the church is God's house (which it is, or ought to be), so the theatre must be the house of the devil. Actors and actresses, too, are not what they often, alas! used to be. Most of them, especially of the higher ranks, are cultivated gentlemen and gentlewomen; and many are very good men and good women, virtuous, domestic, with a high ideal of their art intellectually and morally. So are managers, not a few. Could not these, the wholesome leaven of a corrupt lump, combine to purify the whole lump? Could they not combine to abhor that which is evil, and cleave to that which is good? Better than all the vetoes of the Lord Chamberlain would be an honest lessee, who had the courage to say (as one lessee has been heard to say when urged to accept various French plays), 'There are two sorts of love—one fair, one foul: the latter shall never enter my theatre.' And if, in support of this, our leading actors, or, better, our

actresses—favourites of the public, whom
managers must need propitiate—would absolutely refuse to play such a part as
Marguerite in *La Dame aux Camellias*,
and the countless other parts familiar to
the public, of which the whole interest consists in the breaking, or attempted breaking,
or pardonable and pathetic breaking, of the
seventh commandment — what a change
would at once be made in the atmosphere
of the stage! As great spiritually as that
which is soon to be made materially in
substituting electric light for gas ('airs from
heaven' instead of 'blasts from hell'); for
to many people coming away from a modern
play, as out of the reeking, noxious theatre
where it is acted, is like quitting (in plain
English) a moral hell—a very ingenious,
elegant, amusing hell, but nevertheless as
black as Avernus, and into which the de-
scent is quite as easy.

If a reformation is to come at all, it must come, I believe, *from the women.*

Let those actresses—not few, I trust—who are stainless maidens, faithful wives, good mothers, take their stand—as apparently Miss Anderson does—and refuse to act immoral parts in vicious plays. Let them lead the public taste, instead of weakly following it; refuse to pamper its appetite for anything vile; give it strong, pure, and wholesome food. I believe it would 'swallow' the sternest morality, the highest poetry, if put before it in an attractive form.

There can be no earthly objection to what is called 'stage upholstery.' If the public like *spectacle*, by all means let them have it. A real gem is none the worse for a beautiful setting. The exquisite eye-pictures of the *Winter's Tale* at the Lyceum are truly Shakespearian throughout. Even the slight interpolations of dumb-show crowds, etc., tell exceedingly well. And the world-known parts of Autolycus, Shepherd, and Clown are well sustained by capable actors. But that 'dresses, scenery, and decorations' make the whole of a play is as great a mistake as that the play can do without them.

It remains for Miss Mary Anderson, and perhaps for Mr. Wilson Barrett, who is said to have taken the Globe Theatre, and who, with one or two fatal exceptions, has done more than any manager to raise the tone of the stage—it remains for these, and those like them, to show that under all its feeble, melodramatic, or vicious outside, there is a wholesome inward vitality in our British drama which now survives all foreign taint, and needs no bolstering-up by translations or imitations, but can be both tragic and comic on its own account. Surely it is monstrous that the country which produced

Shakespeare should be obliged to beg, borrow, or steal from other countries the dramatic element which it cannot find itself. It *could* find it if it tried—both plays and actors. Our English stage, like our literature, might be made the greatest and the wholesomest in all the world. We possess good dramatists, good actors, clever managers. Courage only is needed to lead the way; the public would follow like a flock of sheep. That some one will arise and show it is the earnest hope with which the present paper is written.

THE END

P

Printed by R. & R. CLARK, *Edinburgh*